A Gentleman Never Tells

By Eloisa James

A GENTLEMAN NEVER TELLS (a novella)
MY AMERICAN DUCHESS
FOUR NIGHTS WITH THE DUKE
THREE WEEKS WITH LADY X
ONCE UPON A TOWER
AS YOU WISH
WITH THIS KISS (a novella in three parts)
SEDUCED BY A PIRATE (a novella)
THE UGLY DUCHESS
THE DUKE IS MINE
WINNING THE WALLFLOWER (a novella)
A FOOL AGAIN (a novella)
WHEN BEAUTY TAMED THE BEAST
STORMING THE CASTLE (a novella)
A KISS AT MIDNIGHT
A DUKE OF HER OWN
THIS DUCHESS OF MINE
WHEN THE DUKE RETURNS
DUCHESS BY NIGHT
AN AFFAIR BEFORE CHRISTMAS
DESPERATE DUCHESSES
PLEASURE FOR PLEASURE
THE TAMING OF THE DUKE
KISS ME, ANNABEL
MUCH ADO ABOUT YOU
YOUR WICKED WAYS
A WILD PURSUIT
FOOL FOR LOVE
DUCHESS IN LOVE

ELOISA JAMES

A Gentleman Never Tells

A NOVELLA

AVON IMPULSE
An Imprint of HarperCollinsPublishers

Excerpt from *Much Ado About You* copyright © 2005 by Eloisa James.

Excerpt from *A Midsummer Night's Disgrace* appears in *The Official Essex Sisters Companion Guide* copyright © 2016 by Eloisa James, Inc.

EPub Edition JUNE 2016 ISBN: 9780062573063
Print Edition ISBN: 9780062573087
Avon, Avon Impulse, and the Avon Impulse logo are trademarks of HarperCollins Publishers.
10 9 8 7 6 5 4 3

This novella is dedicated to every child who was ever taunted with ugly names— and also to the child who did the bullying. Cruelty cuts both ways.

Acknowledgments

My books are like small children; they take a whole village to get them to a literate state. I want to offer my deep gratitude to my village: my editor, Carrie Feron; my agent, Kim Witherspoon; my Web site designers, Wax Creative; and my personal team: Kim Castillo, Franzeca Drouin, Sharlene Martin Moore, and Anne Connell. In addition, people in many departments of HarperCollins, from Art to Marketing to PR, have done a wonderful job of getting this novella into readers' hands: my heartfelt thanks goes to each of you.

Chapter One

August 13, 1826
Telford Manor
Fontwell, Sussex

"I WOULD PREFER to take supper on a tray." Lizzie didn't look up from her book, because meeting her sister's eyes would only encourage her.

She should have known Catrina wouldn't back down. "Lizzie Troutt, your husband died over a year ago."

"Really?" Lizzie murmured, turning a page. "How time flies." In fact, Adrian had died eighteen months, two weeks, and four days ago.

In his mistress's bed.

"*Lizzie*," Cat said ominously, sounding more like an older sister—which she was—with every word, "if you don't get out of that bed, I shall drag you out. By your hair!"

Lizzie felt a spark of real annoyance. "You already dragged me to your house for this visit. The least you could do is to allow me to read my book in peace."

"Ever since you arrived yesterday, all you've done is read!" Cat retorted.

"I like reading. And forgive me if I point out that Tolbert is not precisely a hotbed of social activity." Cat and her husband, Lord Windingham, lived deep in Suffolk, in a dilapidated manor house surrounded by fields of sheep.

"That is precisely why we gather friends for dinner. Lord Dunford-Dale is coming tonight, and I need you to even the numbers. That means getting up, Lizzie. Bathing. Doing your hair. Putting on a gown that hasn't been dyed black would help. You look like a dispirited crow, if you want the truth."

Lizzie didn't want the truth. In fact, she felt such a stab of anger that she had to fold her lips tightly together or she would scream at Cat.

It wasn't her sister's fault. It wasn't anyone's fault except for her late husband's, and he was definitely late—i.e., dead.

"I know you feel ashamed to be in company," her sister continued, energetically digging her own grave, as far as Lizzie was concerned. "Unfortunately, most people are aware the circumstances of your marriage, not to mention the fact that Adrian was so imprudent as to die away from home."

That was one way of putting it.

Imprudent.

"You make it sound as if he dropped a tea cup," Lizzie observed, unable to stop herself. "I would call the fact that Adrian died in the act of tupping Sadie Sprinkle inconsiderate in the extreme."

"I refuse to allow you to wither away in bed simply because your husband was infatuated with Shady Sadie," Cat said, using the term by which the gossip rags had referred to Adrian's mistress. "You must put all that behind you. Sadie has another protector, and you are out of mourning. It's time to stop hiding."

"I am not hiding," Lizzie said, stung. "I take fresh air and moderate exercise every day. I simply like reading in bed. Or in a chair."

Or anywhere else, to tell the truth. Reading in a peaceful garden was an excellent way to take fresh air.

"Moderate exercise," her sister said with palpable loathing. "You used to ride every day, for pleasure. We would practice archery on a fine day like this, or roam about the countryside, not sit inside reading."

"Adrian's stables were part of the entail, and went to his cousin," Lizzie said, turning the page. She hadn't read a word, but she was hoping that a show of indifference would drive her sister from the room.

"Not the mare that Papa gave you when you turned fourteen!" her sister gasped.

Showing masterly control, Lizzie didn't roll her eyes. "A wife has no true possessions," she said flatly. "Under the law, they belong to her husband and Perdita was, therefore, transferred to the heir."

"Oh, Lizzie," Cat said, her voice woeful.

"It wasn't so terrible," Lizzie said, meaning it. "I went to the auction, and Perdita went to a family with a young girl. I'm certain that she is well cared for and happy."

"Do you realize that by staying home and wearing mourning, you give the illusion that you are grieving for your husband?"

Lizzie's hands tightened around her book. "Do you know what being a widow entails, Cat?"

"Wearing ugly black dresses for the rest of your natural life?"

"It means that I never again need put myself under the control of a man—*any* man. So, no, I have no interest in joining you at dinner. I know perfectly well that Lord Dimble-Dumble has been summoned to audition as my next husband. I don't want him. I'd be more likely to come to dinner if you had invited the butcher."

"I couldn't do that," Cat said, in a sudden digression. "Mr. Lyddle has developed a most unfortunate addiction to strong ale, and he's regularly found lying about in the gutter singing, rather than butchering meat."

"Who does the butchering now?" Lizzie asked, instantly deciding to take a walk to the village and see this interesting musical event herself.

"His wife. My housekeeper says that she gets better cuts at a lower price. You're trying to distract me with talk of singing drunkards," Cat said, unfairly. "Let's discuss your future."

"Let's not."

"We might begin with the fact that you were never in

love with Adrian." Cat began walking around the bed-chamber, waving her hands as she waxed eloquent about her late brother-in-law's flaws.

She was preaching to the choir, so Lizzie stopped listening and just watched Cat pace back and forth. How could it be that her older sister was positively frothing with life and energy and passion, while Lizzie felt like a tired, pale shadow?

Her hand crept toward her book. It wasn't the most interesting novel in the world, but it had the inexpressible charm of being new.

Over the last eighteen months, Lizzie had read every novel she owned three times over. She would be quickly bankrupted if she bought more than two books a week, so one of the best things about visiting Telford Manor was access to her sister's library.

Cat appeared to be hopeless at arranging a refurbishment of the manor—which desperately needed it—but she was very good at ordering novels. And clothing. If Lizzie looked like a black crow, Cat was a chic French peacock.

Lizzie raised her knees, surreptitiously propped her book against them, and slipped back in the story of Eveline, a sixteen-year-old girl being forced to marry an old man. She herself had been twenty when she walked down the aisle.

On the shelf.

Beggars can't be choosers, her father had told her.

Her book suddenly vanished. "No reading!"

Cat was holding the novel above her head, for all the

world as if they were children again. Lizzie used to hope that some day she'd grow up to be as commanding as her sister, but she had given up that idea long ago.

It wasn't just a question of height. Her sister was the type of person who gathered everyone in a room around her, and Lizzie was the type of person whom they walked over on their way to be with Cat.

That sounded resentful, but Lizzie didn't actually feel bitter. She would hate to be the center of attention. She wound her arms around her knees and propped her chin on them. "Cat, may I have my book back, please? It was a hard journey, and I'm tired."

"What do you mean, a hard journey? It can't have taken more than a day and a half!"

"My coach is over twenty years old and the springs are worn out. It bounced so hard on the post road that I couldn't keep my eyes on the page, and my tailbone still hurts."

"If your jointure won't extend to a new vehicle, Joshua or Papa would be happy to buy you a coach."

Lizzie turned her head, putting her right cheek on her knees, and closed her eyes. "No."

She heard her sister drop into the chair by the side of the bed. Then she heard a sigh. "Papa is getting old, Lizzie. He made a terrible mistake, and he knows it. He misses you. If you would just pay him a visit . . ."

"No."

Why would she visit the father who had turned her away when she ran to him in desperation? The father who had known precisely what a disaster her marriage would be, but didn't bother to warn her?

An hour or so after their wedding ceremony, Adrian had brought Lizzie, still wrapped in her bridal veil, to his mother's faded, musty house, and informed her that he had no intention of living with her.

Not only that, but he was late to meet his lover for tea.

It had happened almost six years ago, but she could still remember her stupefaction. She'd been such a silly goose.

"But where do you live?" she had stammered.

"I bought Sadie a house, and we live there," Adrian had said casually. When she frowned in confusion, he had added impatiently, "*Sadie*. Didn't your father tell you her name?"

"Sadie?"

For the first time—and in her experience, the last time—her husband had been a little defensive, even a trifle ashamed. "I never lied. He knows perfectly well that we shall lead separate lives."

"Perhaps you should explain to me," Lizzie had said, "because my father unaccountably forgot to mention it. As did you, I might add."

Adrian had unemotionally laid out the terms of her marriage. It seemed her father had paid a great deal of money for the title of Lady Troutt. For his part, Adrian had wed her for her dowry, and because he needed someone to care for his mother.

"The estate is entailed," he had told her, glancing around the dark sitting room. "It goes to some distant cousin, along with the title, of course. I told your father that I wouldn't be averse to trying for a child, once we've had time to get used to each other."

Lizzie had just gaped at him.

"But we can't bother with that now," Adrian had told her briskly. "Sadie is upset about this mess, naturally enough. I promised her I'd be home by four. My mother takes her luncheon on a tray. There are a couple of maids, but it would be good if you could bring it in yourself. She complains of being lonely."

After that, he left.

A few minutes later, Lizzie left as well. She went home.

Only to be sent back to her husband's house.

There was no point in revisiting her father's line of reasoning. Suffice it to say that no woman—even one who had abundant sensuality and beauty, which Lizzie did not—was capable of seducing a man who didn't return to the house for a fortnight.

A man who doesn't bother to consummate his marriage until he's suffered a heart seizure and has, as the vulgar might put it, been given notice to quit.

A man who despises his lower-class wife, and never bothers to hide it.

Chapter Two

The same day
North Riding
Yorkshire

"YOU'RE NOTHING BUT a stodgy old *twig*!"

The Honorable Oliver Berwick stared at the tip of his boots while he waited for his niece to run out of air.

Or insults.

"If Aunt Augusta had known what you were like, she would never have left her money to you," Hattie cried, with all the passionate emphasis of Ophelia rejecting her former swain in favor of a riverbed.

At that, Oliver raised his eyes. "Are you implying that she might have left her fortune to you? You were in the nursery when she died, Hattie. I don't believe you ever met."

"She would have done better to leave it to a home for cats and dogs."

"We would be in trouble in that case," he pointed out. "Aunt Augusta's money has paid for the roof over our head, your boarding school, and the gown you're wearing, not to mention your pearl drops."

"I suppose you think that I should be grateful to you," Hattie spat.

Oliver knew better than to agree, so he held his tongue.

"I'm not grateful!" she cried. "All I want—all I've asked for in *years*—is to go to the very first house party to which I've been invited. I simply can't understand why you are so unwilling!"

Oliver was back to staring at his boots. "I do not care for the acquaintance."

At fifteen, Hattie was a mercurial, laughing minx one minute, an enraged dictator the next. In either mood, she was adorable, with a mop of curls and sky-blue eyes. Most of the time, he couldn't imagine why her parents had decided to leave her behind in England.

But leave her they did: overcome by missionary fervor, Mr. and Mrs. Sloane had sailed to Egypt and from thence to darkest Africa, leaving their daughter on the doorstep of an uncle who had scarcely known her until a few months ago. What's more, they had pledged to give ten years to the mission.

"Just tell me *why* we can't go," Hattie begged, waving her hands in a gesture that would have done Ophelia proud.

He was going to have to tell her.

Something must have showed in his face, because she pounced like a tabby with a limping mouse. "I'll just keep asking and asking until you do. You know I won't give up, Uncle Oliver. I never do."

On second thought, he knew exactly why her parents had fled to Africa.

He turned and walked over to a chair and dropped into it. This would be humiliating, so he might as well sit down.

Hattie ran after him and sat down as well. "There's a secret afoot!" she crowed. With one of her lightning-quick changes of mood, she wasn't angry any longer and her eyes were bright with curiosity. "I promise not to tell," she said encouragingly.

"When I was young, but old enough to know far better," Oliver said, feeling like an octogenarian, "I behaved like a complete ass."

Hattie's eyes blinked comically. "*You*?" she exclaimed. "How can that possibly be?"

He narrowed his eyes, and she burst into giggles. "It's as if you think you're a saint, so puritanical that it's impossible to imagine you otherwise."

"I am a saint, comparatively speaking."

Hattie's eyes grew round. "You had an illegitimate baby, didn't you? Or rather, the woman whom you betrayed did?"

"No, I—"

"You are *so* lucky that my mama didn't find that out," she cried. "Ever since she grew so religious, she can't abide fornicators."

"Where did you learn that word?" Oliver asked with a frown. "And no, I have no bastard children."

"*There's* a word you're not supposed to use in front of me," Hattie replied cheerfully. "Fornicators appear in the Bible, didn't you know that? I think they turn into salt. Or something along those lines. But 'bastard' is strictly forbidden."

"I gather your mother hasn't managed to pass on her knowledge of the Bible," Oliver observed. His sister had turned to the church after she lost her infant son and, rather to his dismay, had only grown more fervent as time went by.

"Oh, Mama doesn't worry about me," Hattie said. "She says that everyone in England will end up in the blessed Holy Land. Though she might change her mind about you, if she thought you were discussing your bastards in front of me."

"I haven't any children," Oliver said, exasperated. "Look, when I was a young man, I made some friends. We thought making up witty names for people made us appear clever."

"Ooo, Bad Uncle! Do I know your friends?"

"No, you do not. On a few, very rare occasions, we were humorous, but most of the time, we made people laugh by saying cruel things."

His niece chewed her lip. Oliver was surprised how much it hurt to see disappointment in her eyes. Hattie was right to be disillusioned.

"The hostess of this house party, Lady Windingham, was a victim of mine—or rather of the group I belonged to."

"'A victim,'" Hattie repeated. "For goodness' sake, Uncle, how horrid were you?"

"When Lady Windingham debuted, we coined the term the 'Wooly Breeder.' Her father had made a great deal of money sheep-farming and she has a quantity of curly hair."

Hattie's brows drew together. "That *is* horrid. Why on earth would you do something like that? Did she insult you?"

"Actually, I have never met her. I did not come up with the phrase, but I was partly responsible for its spread through society." His friend Charles Darlington had come up with most of the clever little verbal daggers they had used in an effort to sound sophisticated.

But Oliver knew he was as culpable as Darlington. He hadn't just stood by silently; he'd dined out on the strength of their joint cleverness.

"She wasn't the only one," he said, making a clean breast of it. "We called another young lady the 'Scottish Sausage' and that label also became widely known."

"You should not have done that," Hattie stated.

"You are absolutely correct. It was idiotic and cruel. Unfortunately, that sort of casual brutality was fashionable back then. We didn't come up with the term 'Silly Billy' for James Bellingworth, but we might as well have. He's known by it to this day, poor chap."

"Has the 'Scottish Sausage' left that nickname behind?" Hattie asked hopefully.

"Yes. Our foolish name-calling didn't affect her marital prospects; she married the Earl of Mayne in her first season. But Lady Windingham's father had to take her to the country to escape being called a 'Wooly Breeder.' I heard a rumor that a suitor had backed away from his proposal."

"I know what Mother would say." Hattie eyed him.

"I am not a church-going man," Oliver stated, nipping that idea in the bud.

His niece shook her finger at him, for all the world like a disapproving nanny. "No, no, Mama would say that you need to atone for your sins."

"I can hardly marry the lady to make up for the insult," he pointed out. "The next year she married Lord Windingham, who is of far higher rank than I. I'm not sure how you atone for being a pestilent fool, other than sparing the lady the sight of your face."

Over the years, Oliver had gone to absurd lengths to ensure that he didn't come face-to-face with the two women he'd insulted. They had the right to spit in his face, if they met him.

It might make him feel better if they did.

"You are no longer a pestilent fool, Uncle." Mattie leaned forward, patted his knee, and said kindly, "You're rather old, which means you ought to get married, so you have someone to be with you after I leave home, but you're not *pestilent*."

Rather old? Well, he was in his thirties. Thirty-three. That was old to a fifteen-year-old. "I'll take your advice under consideration," he said, dismissing the idea immediately.

"What changed you, Uncle Oliver?" she asked, cock-ing her head. "You're no longer cantankerous, as far as I know. My mama imposed on you terribly by leaving me here. But you've never said a cross word about her."

"I like you," Oliver said. "When you're not sniping at me, you're good company."

"When did you stop being clever and become the very nice fellow you are now?"

"Very nice fellow" was slightly better than "rather old," but Oliver didn't care for either description.

"Before I inherited Aunt Augusta's estate and her coal mine, I was merely a younger son, with just enough money to do nothing. That's a dangerous state of affairs, given as I was manifestly unsuited to the church, and I couldn't see myself in the army either."

"If you'd gone into the army, you'd be married by now," Hattie pronounced. "Girls cannot resist a red uniform, in particular. But to return to my point, you ought to make amends for your ill behavior, no matter how young you were at the time. Mother would say that your soul is in danger."

He must have looked unconvinced, because she added, "I expect the fact that you've never atoned for your sins explains your bachelor state!"

"How so?" Oliver asked.

"Guilt," she explained. "Unless you apologize to Lady Windingham, you will die alone. *All* alone. I am remarkably fond of you, Uncle, but I fully intend to marry and move away. Just in case you thought that I will always live with you."

"I did not think that," Oliver said, managing to choke

back the fact that he found living with a fifteen-year-old girl to be sufficient penance for any number of sins he may have committed.

"You will grow more and more lonely every year," Hattie said, clasping her hands together. "Your soul will shrivel and your heart grow harder, hard, *so* hard. Black as black can be."

"You don't think you're overdoing it a bit?" Oliver inquired.

"Absolutely not! Mother has some phrase she uses, something about a canker in the rose, or a . . ." She trailed off. "You know how Mother is; she has a Bible verse for every thought. The only one I can ever remember is 'Jesus wept.'"

"Not very useful," Oliver agreed.

"My point is that you can apologize at Lady Windingham's house party. Obviously, *she* has forgiven you, because the invitation is addressed to both of us. But in order for *you* to do the same for yourself, you must ask for forgiveness. In person."

Oliver had the idea that Hattie's best friend had twisted her stepmother's arm until poor Lady Windingham had no choice but to invite him.

Still, it wasn't a terrible idea.

He didn't think about the whole thing often, but when he did, he would wince and swear at himself. Maybe a few times a year. Perhaps once a month.

"All right," he said, giving in. "I suppose we can go."

"Excellent," Hattie said, beaming at him. "I shall take care of everything, Uncle. You mustn't worry." She patted him on the knee again. Apparently, he was too doddering to handle travel arrangements himself.

"When is this house party?" Oliver asked, moving his legs so as to discourage further patting.

"In a fortnight," she said brightly. "Telford Manor is in Sussex. I already asked your coachman, and he estimates it will be a seven-day journey. I'm very good company in a coach. My parents always said so."

She patted his knee again.

Chapter Three

By the time they reached Telford Manor, in the late afternoon two weeks later, Oliver was thoroughly sympathetic with his sister's decision to travel to Egypt.

Hell, she was probably lying in a hammock by the River Nile with a refreshing drink in her hand, happily musing over her escape from the most irritating girl who ever existed.

By the time Hattie's mother returned to England, Hattie would be a mature and agreeable twenty-five. In fact, his sister's missionary fervor was probably just a sibling revenge plot.

"How much time has passed?" Hattie asked, throwing herself across the carriage seat to look out the other window. Again.

"Eight minutes since you last inquired," he answered, not looking up from the book he was attempting to read.

Hattie believed that books were old-fashioned, and

she would rather talk. Unfortunately, her subjects of conversation were limited to her thoughts and feelings on any given subject. After weeks of extremely close proximity, Oliver could anticipate her feelings on any subject, so there was little to discover by further dialogue.

She liked pretty dresses, and pretty trees, and pretty sheep. She disliked anything that reminded her of mud, or rain, or less pretty animals. She positively hated anything dirty. Horses joined that list after she ruined a pair of favorite slippers stepping into dung.

Pimples were apparently the work of the devil (she cited her mother's authority on this point), and not the result of eating two chocolate puddings at one sitting, as Oliver had suggested.

Olivier thought that carriages were the work of the devil. That, and whoever had invented the stupid idea of holding house parties in godforsaken parts of England.

"There are so many sheep in the world," Hattie observed. "That field looks as if it's full of white buttercups, if there is such a thing as a white buttercup. Ooh, look, there's a lamb! It's *so* pretty . . . no, it's too late. Really, Uncle Oliver, you should put that book down and look out the window so you don't miss everything."

When the vehicle finally drew into a cobblestone courtyard, Hattie erupted from the carriage and flew straight through the open front door of the manor house. Oliver climbed down and stretched.

Telford Manor, home of Lord Windingham and his wife, was an old, comfortable house made of red herringbone bricks, with sloping roofs going in all directions.

Unlike his niece, Oliver felt markedly reluctant to enter the house, never mind the fact that a butler stood in the doorway waiting for him.

His coachman was consulting with the stablemaster about returning the horses to the posting inn in Ashington. "Everything all right here?" Oliver said, joining them.

"Snug and tight, sir," his coachman said, turning back to his conversation. "Now, then, Mr. Puttle, let's get these horses into the stables, shall we? We'll rest them overnight and I'll take them back in the morning."

With no further manly exchange to be had, there was only one option, so Oliver marched into the house and surrendered to the butler, whose name turned out to be Bartleby.

"May I relieve you of your overcoat, sir?" Bartleby asked.

Oliver was thinking that perhaps he should return those horses himself. He could turn about and head for the posting house and return on horseback in a few days. He could give the household time to prepare.

To get used to the idea.

He could get used to the idea.

"What happened to my niece?" he asked Bartleby, who was silently waiting for him to make up his mind. Good butlers were like that. They seemed to know what was going through your head before you did.

Bloody annoying, if you thought about it.

"Miss Windingham escorted Miss Sloane to a chamber, so that she might refresh herself after the drive. Lady Windingham would be pleased if you joined her in the drawing room, or, if you wish, I can bring you to your chamber."

"I shall greet her ladyship first," Oliver said. He might as well get the initial meeting over with. Not that he meant to blurt out an apology immediately. He had to choose the right moment.

"If you would follow me, sir, I shall announce you."

"Right," he said, squaring his shoulders.

The drawing room had to be a quarter mile long, and the only thing that stopped it from resembling Versailles was that half the gilt paint had been rubbed off the mirrors. Well, that, and a mirror or two had gone missing, leaving only ten or eleven on each wall.

He crossed an acre of well-worn carpet before he reached two women sitting by the fire, both of whom rose to their feet as he approached.

Too late, Oliver remembered that he hadn't the faintest idea what his hostess looked like. He should have asked the butler, but the man had peeled away after bellowing his name.

The woman closest to him was far too young, in her mid-twenties, if that.

She had sunshine-colored hair piled up on her head, high cheekbones, and a straight nose. But it was her mouth that made him stutter-step.

It was generous and wide, with a deep, rosy bottom lip. It made a man long to see her smile.

All the same, there was something a little haunted about her face. Sad, perhaps. She looked tired and withdrawn. And she was dressed in mourning.

Obviously, Lady Windingham had to be the other woman. She had even more hair and was almost as tall as he was. In fact, it could be that all her piled-up hair gave her the advantage.

She stepped forward with a twinkling smile and said, "Mr. Berwick, I am happy to meet you. May I introduce my younger sister, Lady Troutt? The remainder of our party will arrive in two days."

He bowed before each lady and kissed their hands, as her words sunk in. "*Two days?*"

"I must apologize for my daughter; I gather that the girls wished some time to themselves before other guests arrived, so they perpetrated something of a conspiracy. Sarah was asked to write out the invitations, and she altered the date on yours."

No wonder Hattie had trotted straight into the house; she didn't want to be there when he discovered why she had offered to handle the travel arrangements.

"Please, do join us," Lady Windingham said, with another charming smile. She seated herself, poured a cup of tea, and handed it over.

She didn't seem to be holding a grudge, so Oliver decided he'd been an ass to worry about the past. They were all grown-ups, after all.

He accepted a crumpet, and then watched as Lady Windingham tried to talk her sister into eating one.

Thank God, Oliver thought irreverently, Troutt didn't woo his future wife during the year of Darlington's rule over polite—or impolite—society. With that incredible mouth . . .

After another glance at her lips, he hastily stuffed his mouth with crumpet. Lady Troutt was exquisite, and even the fact that her eyes were etched with weariness did not tame his body's reaction to her.

Damn it, the woman was probably newly widowed. He wouldn't know; he hadn't been to London in two years, and he never bothered to read the society pages.

She finally added a crumpet to her plate, throwing her sister a small but enchanting smile.

Oliver cleared his throat. "I regret to see that you are in mourning, Lady Troutt." He paused.

She looked at him with clear, expressionless eyes. "Yes. I am a widow."

Her sister made a noise that sounded like a snort. Perhaps some tea went down the wrong way.

"I am sorry for your loss," Oliver said.

"Yes, well," Lady Troutt said. "As everyone knows, I am better off this way."

What an extraordinary statement. Oliver looked at her with some perplexity. If he had been her husband, he'd have made damn sure that she would mourn him after he was gone.

"Lizzie," Lady Windingham said reprovingly, "poor Mr. Berwick hasn't the faintest idea what you're talking about."

Lizzie was a rather jolly name for someone so reserved and wan.

She scowled at her older sister in a not-jolly way. "You said that everyone knew."

"Knew?" Oliver inquired, feeling as if he'd walked into a theater at intermission. "Knew what?"

"The circumstances of my husband's death," the lady said.

She had scarcely nibbled the crumpet, he noticed, even though she was too thin.

"Was your husband killed in that boat that went down in the Bay of Biscay?" he asked, thinking of the most notorious accident in recent history.

"No. The details of Lord Troutt's passing are disagreeable, and better forgotten."

She had a crooked smile that made something in him snarl. Lizzie was meant to be laughing in the sun, not pale and thin.

Wait.

What was her name? *Troutt?*

He blinked and his eyes widened before he caught himself.

The lady's shoulders slumped, almost imperceptibly, before she pulled her slim figure erect once again. "I see that the circumstances of Lord Troutt's demise have come to mind," she said composedly.

"I told you so," her sister put in. She was buttering another crumpet. "Unfortunately, your husband was the toast of the majority of gentlemen in Britain."

Oliver did remember reading about Troutt's demise in the arms of one of the best-known courtesans in all England. There had been ballads written to his prowess, and many a joke dedicated to his supposedly happy ending.

"He was a fool," Oliver growled. He had seen Shady Sadie singing in a revue once. She was a fleshy, glittering type of woman. A simple woman.

Lady Troutt was complicated in the way that a violin concert is complicated. She looked cautious and sensual, at the same time.

"I think we can all agree with that assessment," Lady Windingham said, taking a last bite of her second crumpet.

He'd guess that Lizzie was designed by nature to have a figure as rounded as her sister's, but she was slim.

Not slim: thin. Too thin.

It was none of his business, but for some reason, it made him restless. He'd like to coax her into eating, like a baby bird fallen from its nest.

Yet she was no baby. Her dress was made of tired fabric that pulled tight against her bosom.

She reached out for the cup of tea and lust darted through his body again.

Bloody hell. How long had it been since Troutt died?

Not that it mattered.

He'd made up his mind long ago not to marry, and Hattie's warning about the peril of dying alone hadn't changed his mind.

Lizzie Troutt was definitely the kind of woman whom a man marries.

Therefore, he should stay far away from her.

"May I offer you a slice of this cake?" he said instead, leaning toward her. It was her eyes: hazel with little flecks of green. He wanted to see them smiling.

She didn't smile.

Or eat the cake.

Chapter Four

"HOW CAN YOU possibly refuse dinner?" Cat was gaping
as if Lizzie had announced she was moving to India.

"I have a headache," Lizzie said. Falsely. She was comfortably seated by the fireplace in her chamber, and her
head felt fine.

She just didn't want to look at Oliver Berwick for more
than two minutes, and definitely not with a glass of wine
in her hand.

He was so handsome that he made her teeth ache.

Cat leaped out of the chair opposite, her body vibrat-
ing with frustration. "Last month, when I was in London,
you refused to join us at the theater, although you used
to love watching a play. You wouldn't come to a musicale,
or a ball, or anything. And now you won't even come to
dinner?"

"I do not choose to go into company," Lizzie observed.
"I prefer a quiet life." At the moment, she longed to snatch

up her sister's collection of novels, cart them out to her elderly carriage, and trundle away home.

That wasn't a bad idea, actually.

Rosy color was rising in Cat's cheeks, always a bad sign. "You wouldn't even come to my house to have tea with my closest friend, and you know how much I want you to meet Josie!"

Lizzie had no interest in meeting a countess, let alone the wife of the notorious Earl of Mayne. She had read a book that described all of Mayne's conquests, a scandalous tome entitled *The Earl of Hellgate, or Night Scenes Among the Ton*. She was no Puritan, but she didn't approve.

Though honesty forced her to admit that she'd read every page of that memoir, and some of them twice.

Cat gave her a squinty frown. "Josie is my best friend, and you've repeatedly avoided meeting her. She will join us in two days, and if you refuse to get out of bed during her visit, I'll swear I will drag you out by your hair."

"Of course, I will greet Lady Mayne," Lizzie said, exhausted by the whole conversation. She wasn't looking forward to being the object of a countess's sympathy.

Cat had always had interesting friends, even in school. She was a bit wild, and sometimes loud, but always interesting. But Lizzie never got along with her sister's group: she was too shy, too aware of being a cit's daughter, too much of a bookworm.

"You're like some sort of hibernating hedgehog," Cat said darkly. "You can't hide in your chamber forever."

Lizzie begged to differ. She had absolutely no problem hibernating until she felt like emerging, whether that happened tomorrow or never.

"You even dress as if you were on the wrong side of sixty," Cat continued, when Lizzie didn't respond. "What has changed you so much, Lizzie?" She dropped onto the settee. "You can't pretend that you are grieving for Adrian. You are a rich widow with your whole life ahead of you, so why aren't you enjoying yourself?"

Rich she wasn't, though Lizzie didn't feel like sharing the fact that she'd sold Adrian's unentailed property and set up a fund for his son. Her solicitor had discovered that the boy had been dropped in an orphanage soon after Shady Sadie went on to her next protector.

The very thought made fury burn up her spine. She was angry at Adrian. And angry at Sadie. That rage made her start from her chair and blurt out what she'd never told anyone.

"I could forget the fact that Adrian married me for my dowry," she said in a low voice, her fists clenching. "I could forget the fact that he justified his actions by announcing to all and sundry that Father was a cit who traded a wallflower daughter for a title. Do you want to know what I can't forget, Cat? Do you?"

"Yes, I do want to know," her sister said, her eyes steady. "What is possibly worth being so angry about that you plan to hide indoors for the rest of your life?"

Lizzie opened her mouth . . . and looked away. "It's not worth discussing."

"You must. It's like poison inside you. You have to tell someone." Cat reached up and pulled her back onto the settee beside her.

Lizzie had the feeling her sister was right, so she forced the words out of her mouth. "Four months after his heart seizure, Adrian decided it was time to consummate our marriage."

From the corner of her eye, she saw Cat make a sharp movement.

"He was not able to become stiff enough to do the deed." The words proved as painful to say aloud as they were to think about.

"Let me guess," Cat snarled. "He blamed you for that failure."

"He was very nice about it, actually," Lizzie said. "He was accustomed to a woman with a generous bosom. I got the impression that Sadie resembles the top half of an hourglass."

Cat's brows drew together. "Probably a dairy cow. He was such a dolt."

"Adrian liked—" Lizzie broke off.

"Go on," Cat said grimly. "Tell me every word the Royal Wart told you."

"He just . . . you see, Sadie is quite vivacious."

"He didn't introduce you to Shady Sadie!" Cat's voice rose.

"Oh, no!" Lizzie said hastily. "But he used to talk about her when . . . when he was home."

That wasn't often, especially after his mother died. The last year of their marriage she saw him twice.

"So what did he say about this paragon of womanhood?"

"It wasn't so much about *her*, as about the difference

between us," Lizzie said, figuring she might as well make a clean breast of it. "He suggested a few things I might do to get him more aroused, and I declined. I felt incredible relief when it became clear that Adrian couldn't manage an erection with me."

"What woman wouldn't?" Cat said, with a shiver.

"But since he died, I've grown to be so angry. And humiliated. I know it's not rational."

"I'd be livid. He wanted *you* to do things to get *him* aroused? It should have been the other way around. He should have knelt at your feet, thanking you for even considering bedding such a man as he."

"He was my husband," Lizzie said. "What was I supposed to do? Run home?" Those words hung in the air for a moment.

"You could have come to me."

"Adrian wasn't all that bad," Lizzie said, reaching for her sister's hand and giving it a squeeze.

"How dare he convince you that you were inadequate?" Cat looked as if she was ready to topple Adrian's tombstone.

"Do you know what he reminded me of when he had his clothes off?" Lizzie said, realizing that she did feel better for blurting it all out.

Cat's nose wrinkled. "I'm not sure I want to know."

"Oh, not *that* part. The rest of him. Do you remember that fat, hairy pig that Mr. Murgatroyd kept in his back garden?"

"Ugh!"

"It wasn't the belly as much as the attitude. Mr. Murgatroyd's pig used to root around in the mud with the certainty that the world owed him a carrot every morning."

"Why on earth would you believe it when a hairy trotter told you that you were unattractive, which is a complete and total lie, by the way?"

"I had two seasons. There was plenty of chances for other men to convince me of my charms."

"Not after Adrian made it clear that you were his," Cat said grimly.

"What do you mean?"

"Joshua told me that Adrian told his entire club—which included most of the young men in London—that he claimed you. So no, he had no competition in your second season, at least."

Lizzie shrugged. "Adrian called me a tiresome country mouse, and he was right. I have no conversation, and no jokes, and I don't even have breasts to speak of."

Cat opened her mouth, but Lizzie raised her hand. "To go back to the subject, I'm sorry I declined to meet your friend the countess for tea. I just couldn't imagine that we'd have much in common."

"You will love her! We talk for hours whenever we manage to see each other."

"She's got a little girl, doesn't she? And you have two little boys, not to mention your stepdaughter. I don't have any children, and I'm not going to have any. Much though I adore my nephews, I'd rather be reading than talking about children."

"Rather be reading!" Cat burst out, coming to her feet. "Is there anything in the world you'd rather do than read?"

Lizzie didn't need to think about that twice. "No."

"This is Adrian Troutt's fault! You are exquisite, even now, when you're too thin. You look just like Mother." Cat put her hands on her hips and scowled magnificently, as if she could change the world by willing it so.

Lizzie looked up at her sister, making sure that Cat understood the importance of what she was about to say. "I will never again put my happiness in the hands of a man who may well be lying through his teeth. *Never.*"

"Not every man is a liar."

"I have as much money as I need to live comfortably and buy books," Lizzie said firmly. "I do not like dressing for dinner and eating seven courses. I have never been comfortable in polite society, despite Father's decision to trade my happiness for a title."

"You're giving his actions the worst possible connotation. Papa genuinely thought that Adrian would not be able to resist you."

Lizzie snorted.

"When it became clear that Adrian preferred Shady Sadie, particularly after he boasted all over town about the birth of his son, Papa was devastated. He had bet on the fact that Adrian would find you irresistible, and he lost."

"I can't imagine why he ever thought that plan would work."

Cat sat down beside her again. "Because you're beautiful, dear, even if you don't see it."

More than anything, Lizzie wanted to return to the warm nest of her little blue bedchamber back in London.

After Adrian's mother died, she had the back bedroom renovated and made it her own.

No more lying in a matrimonial bed that had never, even for one night, held more than one body. Luckily for her, the distant cousin who inherited Adrian's estate had no interest in the house; she paid him a nominal rent.

But she had promised to stay with Cat for at least a fortnight. "All right," she said with a sigh. "I'll stay. But no matchmaking. Perhaps I'll join you at dinner."

By the time the evening rolled around, she was deep in her book. Eveline's ancient fiancé had taken himself off to the Crusades, leaving his future bride vulnerable to kidnappers.

Lizzy didn't come down to dinner.

Chapter Five

OLIVER ENTERED THE drawing room that evening with a mission. He meant to apologize to his hostess, and after that . . . well, after that, he meant to persuade Lizzie Troutt to eat her supper. Or at least enough to support a grown woman.

Not such a large goal.

When he was upstairs bathing—and later, when he was yelling at Hattie for fibbing about the dates of the house party—he couldn't stop thinking about the little droop at the corners of Mrs. Troutt's lush mouth. The way her cheekbones were drawn tight.

It wasn't right.

Unfortunately, the lady was nowhere to be seen, but Lady Windingham was standing by the side of the room, talking to the butler.

He walked over, discovering that his hostess was eating olives, one after another, as if they were grapes.

The girls were seated beside her, chattering between themselves.

"If you'll forgive me," he said, bowing, "I wonder if I might have a private word."

"Why don't we take a promenade?" She said, tucking her hand into his elbow. "At least it will stop me from eating every olive in the house. Do you ever find yourself craving one type of food so much that you would kill for it?"

"No," Oliver said. He had the sudden, absurd thought that he might kill to see Lizzie Troutt naked.

"This room is so monstrously large," Lady Windingham said cheerfully, "that I tell my husband we should set up a permanent cricket pitch at one end, though we've only got as far as the occasional game of croquet so far."

Croquet indoors?

He pushed the thought away. And, for that matter, the question of what Lizzie Troutt would look like, naked and in his arms. "Lady Windingham, I accepted your invitation to this party, because I have long wished to apologize for my horrendous behavior when you debuted, years ago. I was, and remain, horrified at my dreadful attempts at being clever."

She grinned at him. "Do you know, Mr. Berwick, if a certain gentleman had not backed away from his marriage proposal due to the notoriety of Mr. Darlington's nicknaming me the 'Wooly Breeder'—for Darlington long ago confessed to creating the label—my father would have married me off before the season was over?"

She paused.

"It would not have been a happy match?" Oliver asked.

"The gentleman in question was Viscount de Lesser."

Oliver frowned. "He was a friend of my father's, but surely—"

"The viscount died a few years ago, of a combination of gout and dropsy. I kept an eye on him, because until he took offense to marrying a 'Wooly Breeder,' he was quite enthusiastic about marrying me."

"He must have been already seventy!"

"Seventy-three. My father is fond of calculating odds. He decided that the odds of my husband dying while I was still of breeding age were quite high. Therefore, he chose to trade a year or two of discomfort for the title of viscountess."

It seemed bloody-minded to Oliver, but he could hardly say that aloud. What did he know of daughters, after all?

Still, irritating though Hattie could be, he would no more consider marrying her to an old man than to a beggar.

"It seemed reasonable to my father," Lady Windingham said with a sigh. "Thank goodness Lord Windingham came along the next season. My father is inordinately proud of the fact that both of his daughters hold titles."

Oliver spent most of his time in the north country and rarely bothered to enter polite society, but even he had heard of Troutt's adoration for Shady Sadie, which had to have predated his marriage. "I see," he murmured.

"My father knew of my brother-in-law's relationship with Sadie Sprinkle," the lady said, obviously guessing his thought. "He decided that Troutt's inordinately large girth suggested that he would live only a year or two. He was wrong; my sister had to endure a flagrantly adulterous husband for four years."

"That is truly unfortunate," Oliver said. He couldn't think of any comment on the subject that wouldn't cast a pejorative light on her father, so he said, "I gather you were saved from de Lesser's attentions by Lord Windingham?"

"That is exactly right," she said, giving him another one of her wide-mouthed smiles. "It's family lore at this point, but the very first person I danced with in my second season was my future husband, Joshua. The previous spring he had been in mourning for his first wife and did not come to London."

"So am I to understand that my callow remarks were in the service of fate?" Olivier said, a wave of relief coursing through his body.

"Exactly! I believe my husband will wish to thank you as well."

"Fate cannot excuse the cruelty of my conduct," Oliver said frankly. "I truly apologize, Lady Windingham. I'm sure I wounded you, and I am deeply regretful."

"You were considerably younger than Darlington, weren't you?"

"That is no excuse."

"You're being very nice about it, but Darlington told me a long time ago that it was entirely his doing."

"If there is anything I can do to atone for what I did," Oliver said, rattling off the sentence that Hattie had made him promise to utter, "you have only to ask."

His hostess's eyes narrowed, and she came to a halt.

They had walked a considerable way, so far that the far end of the room seemed shrouded in twilight.

"Do you mean it?" she asked.

"Absolutely." He was tired of feeling shame. It was an exhausting emotion.

"I have need of a knight errant, as it happens."

What? She couldn't possibly be asking for nightly privileges.

She read his eyes and burst into laughter. "You are quite handsome, Mr. Berwick, but I'm afraid that my husband absorbs all my attention." She had charming laughter wrinkles beside her eyes.

Quite suddenly, Oliver discovered that he liked Lady Windingham. Really liked her. Not in that way, but in the way he used to like his sister before the Bible transformed her into such elevated—and judgmental—company.

"Now that I finally have a Lancelot, I have a quest for you," the lady said.

"Anything," Oliver said, meaning it.

"Dear me, I hope all this power doesn't go to my head."

"If I had met you your first season, I would have given Viscount de Lesser a run for his money."

"My father thought first and foremost about titles, so I'm afraid it wouldn't have worked. Besides, we wouldn't have been happy."

"No?"

"Joshua is as calm as the night. No matter what sort of fit I fly into, he is always steady. He's my rock."

"My qualifications on that front are untried," he agreed, taking her arm again as they turned and began walking back toward the fireplace. "So how may I help you, Lady Windingham?"

"First of all, you'd better call me Cat. I can tell that we're going to be great friends. And second, you're going to help me with my sister."

"With Lady Troutt?" he asked, startled.

"Lizzie is a widow, as you know. I want you to get her up on a horse, because she never rides any more, even though she used to love it. And I want you to make her laugh."

It seemed he was right. It wasn't natural for Lizzie Troutt to be so pensive.

"You have two days before everyone arrives, which should be enough," she added.

"Is Lady Troutt grieving for her husband?" It seemed incredible, but stranger things had happened.

"Absolutely not," Cat stated. "Adrian was a miserable cur, who displayed shameful disrespect for his wife."

"I agree."

"You are the perfect person to pull her out of the doldrums because you're so clever. In fact, if you wanted to come up a nickname for Adrian, I would welcome it. Adrian the Anteater, for example."

"I'm out of the business of calling people names," Oliver said.

"Then tell her a funny joke. Lizzie used to scream with laughter at the sort of joke in which a pope dines with the king. Your charge is to make her laugh so hard she cries."

Oliver frowned. He wasn't a joking sort of man.

"I still remember one joke that made us laugh hysterically," Cat said encouragingly. "'Why are blind men like the philosophers Plato, Seneca, and Socrates?'"

"I have no idea," Oliver replied.

"Because they philosophize."

He frowned again.

"Feel-loss-of-eyes," Lady Windingham explained.

"I know no jokes of that sort," he stated categorically.

"It's not just a matter of jokes, Mr. Berwick."

"Oliver," he said.

She smiled at him. "My sister had one of the best seats in the county and she used to love nothing more than going out for a long ride. She adored playing games and she was ferociously competitive. Now she just sits about reading gothic novels."

Oliver nodded.

"I don't suppose you've read any, but Lizzie absolutely adores an author called Lucibella Delicosa. They're the sort of novels in which people are always trying to sleep in a room with an insomniac ghost rattling chains."

"Ah. Those ghosts tend to be awake at the wrong moments."

"They're so impolite, aren't they? I would take a rest and oil my chains. So that's where you come in, Oliver," Cat said. "*You* are going to make Lizzie happy again. You are going to use all that cleverness you honed in your misspent youth to make my sister fall about with laughter."

"I can try."

"I just don't understand why she's so sad, given that her marriage was never a love match," Cat confided.

"I expect she's ashamed," Oliver said. He had some knowledge of that debilitating emotion.

"She has *nothing* to be ashamed of!" Cat cried. "Nothing! All the shame belonged to Adrian the Alligator. No, my father deserves some as well, since he insisted on the marriage. He regrets it now, but it's too late. She hasn't paid him a visit for years."

"On occasion, shame attaches itself where it needn't," Oliver said. "I will do my best."

"That will be more than enough," Cat said with a warm smile.

Oliver had the strangest feeling, as if a rock had lifted off his heart. He had been forgiven for the most dishonorable period of his life, and it felt wonderful. "Lord Windingham is a very lucky man," he said, meaning it.

She wrinkled her nose. "So am I. If I were to calculate the odds the way my father does, I would venture to say that Joshua and I have forty or more happy years ahead of us. I want that the same for my sister, and I have just the right man in mind."

"Who is it?"

"Mr. Benjamin Jagger," Cat said. "You may not know him."

"I do know him. We have both invested in the new railway line at Stockton-on-Tees. He is an excellent man."

Oliver didn't think Ben was a good choice for Lizzie Troutt, though. Jagger was a rough-and-ready sort of fellow, and Cat's sister looked as if she needed delicate handling.

"Mr. Jagger confided to my husband that he intends to marry. So all I have to do is put them together and he's sure to fall in love with Lizzie. Don't you think?"

"Yes," Oliver said slowly. "Yes, of course he will."

Chapter Six

The following afternoon

"ARE WE ALONE for tea?" Lizzie asked. Not that she was interested in Mr. Berwick's whereabouts, because she wasn't. Not at all.

"Joshua took the girls and Mr. Berwick off to see the tour of Madame Tussauds' waxworks that's two villages over. I thought it might make you more melancholy, since most of the exhibit is made up of guillotined members of the French royal family." Cat shuddered.

"I'm not melancholy," Lizzie protested. "I'm quiet. By nature."

Cat handed her a cup of tea. "I'll never forgive Adrian for turning you into a sad, silent ghost. He's the one who's dead, Lizzie, not you."

She hadn't become ghostlike, surely? Lizzie nibbled on a scone. Sometimes she did feel as if she were drifting along, invisible to most people.

"We missed you last night at dinner."

"I enjoyed myself reading," Lizzie said stubbornly. "Besides, I know what you really mean: Mr. Berwick has been invited to audition for the part of my husband."

"No," Cat said baldly. "He only came because young Hattie forced him to."

"Oh," Lizzie said, rather disconcerted. "Well, my point is that the mere idea of handing myself over to another male makes me dizzy. I won't do it."

Cat gave her a hard look over her teacup. "Is this really the life that you want, Lizzie? No babies of your own?"

"Children are so repetitive, aren't they?" Lizzie said apologetically. "It's not that I don't have masses of love for your children, because I do. But I truly don't think I could do it myself. I can't bear the way your nanny speaks to you, let alone them. It's as if she considers you another child."

"That's just Nanny's manner," Cat said philosophically. "She's used to training people and she forgets that Joshua and I are adults. Just think, if you never have a husband or children, someday you'll be all alone. I'm older than you, so I'll die first."

"I might take a lover," Lizzie said. "When I'm an octogenarian, I mean."

Her sister clearly knew how preposterous that suggestion was, since she ignored it all together. "You'll be sitting around in your eighties all in black, and everyone will pity you, because you are still mourning a man who treated you like the dirt under his boot."

"I am wearing violet today," Lizzie pointed out.

Her sister snorted. "Half-mourning. A dress that doesn't show even a hint of *décolletage*. No lace. No flounces. I expect you haven't had a new bonnet since . . . since the funeral!"

Over the years of her marriage, Lizzie had lost interest in clothing. Fashion existed to tempt men, after all. What most ladies didn't understand was that an opera dancer was enticing without wearing a shred of clothing. A proper lady didn't have a hope of keeping a man to herself.

Her brother-in-law Joshua seemed thoroughly smitten with Cat, but she counted him an exception.

"I suppose I could acquire some new clothes," she said, unenthusiastically.

"Does that mean you will give up your blacks *and* your half-mourning?"

"If you insist. Is there a seamstress in the village? I haven't seen the singing butcher, so I might go after tea."

"The butcher has disappeared! Everyone thinks that his wife may have accidentally shot him one night, believing he was a burglar, you understand. And no one feels that a fuss should be made, so that's that."

"I admire her," Lizzie said. "If I was a more forthright person, I could have taken after Adrian with a dueling pistol."

"Only if you cared about him. One doesn't shoot people whom one hardly knows. At any rate, we have no need for the village seamstress. I've been waiting for the right moment to tell you."

"Tell me what?"

"Well, when Sarah and I went to Paris in November, I acquired a gown or two for you."

"You didn't!"

"Yes, I most certainly did. It was easy enough; you're just Sarah's height, if a bit slimmer, and she needed an entirely new wardrobe, appropriate for a young lady who is no longer in school."

"I wish you hadn't," Lizzie said. "I won't be able to repay you."

Her sister's brow darkened. "Don't ever say something like that to me again."

"Well, but—"

"No buts. Joshua has made heaps of money with his steamship. In fact, I've invited one of his partners, Mr. Jagger, to the house party." Cat busied herself by dripping honey on a scone, rather obviously not looking at Lizzie. "You can wear one of the dresses I bought you to dinner with him, and that will be thanks enough."

"You know, in all your matchmaking fervor, you've forgotten the fact that Adrian's death made me notorious," Lizzie pointed out. "Men don't like that sort of thing in a wife."

"You think *you're* notorious?" Cat snorted. "Don't you remember what happened to me in my first season?"

Lizzie frowned. "I was away at school. All I remember is that Joshua took one look at you and fell in love."

"That was my second season; my first was a disaster. I

was labeled the 'Woolly Breeder,' thanks to Papa's sheep farms. I had to be taken back to the country to rusticate in disgrace."

She popped a bite of scone into her mouth, looking completely unperturbed.

Lizzie's understanding was that polite society was made up of people treating each other in astonishingly impolite ways, so she wasn't terribly surprised.

"How horrid that must have been," she said. "Do you think that our hair had something to do with the nickname?" They both had white-blonde corkscrew ringlets that curled so thickly they were hard to pin up. "I have sometimes thought that I resemble a Scottish sheep, the really wooly kind. Perhaps I should shear it off."

"Don't," Cat advised. "My husband adores my hair. My point is that Joshua didn't give a damn what people were calling me. We danced and then he showed up the next morning and asked Papa for my hand."

"Joshua is a prince among men," Lizzie said, letting her tone reveal her suspicion that her brother-in-law was the only man of his ilk.

"I was not the only young woman in the marriage mart bequeathed with an ugly nickname," Cat said, catching a drop of honey on her finger.

Lizzie took another bite of her scone, but it tasted like sawdust and regret, so she put it down. "Oh, yes?"

"Josie was given a horrible label in her first season as well, which gave us an instant bond. Yet now she is happily married to the Earl of Mayne. Public humiliation didn't stop him from marrying her."

Presumably Josie was so beautiful that the earl took one look and fell at her feet, just as Joshua had at Cat's. Unfortunately, no man had ever shown an inclination to sprawl on the ground in front of Lizzie.

"So what was Josie's sobriquet?" she asked.

"Sobriquet? Darling, you really must stop reading so much. It makes you sound like a bluestocking."

Lizzie rolled her eyes.

"The Scottish Sausage," Cat said. "Isn't that dreadful? Between us, I'd rather be a Wooly Breeder. Do you want the last scone, or shall I have it?"

"You have it."

"I'm so hungry that I'm beginning to wonder whether I might be *enceinte* again," Cat confided.

"That would be wonderful!" Lizzie said, meaning it. She didn't want children herself, but she was very fond of her little nephews.

"Odd, though. It's been four years."

"I hope you have a girl next," Lizzie said. "I must say, I think the real oddity is that you and the countess became good friends on the basis of your wretched experiences."

"No, here is the *truly* odd thing. Mr. Berwick— Oliver—is a member of the group who gave me the label Wooly Breeder. He didn't make it up, though. That was Darlington."

Lizzie's mouth fell open. "And you invited him to the house?"

"Well, of course I did," Cat said. "I've never seen the point of holding grudges. That grudge you're holding against your husband is only hurting you."

Lizzie chose to ignore the fiftieth piece of sisterly advice to come her direction in the last day or so. "Do you suppose that Mr. Berwick will grace me with a nickname?"

"The Woeful Widow?" Cat asked. "I doubt it. He apologized in the most magnificent way for his youthful foolishness."

Adrian had never even considered apologizing. Why should he? To his mind, he was practically doing charity work when he married her.

"But now you have a title," he would say, when Lizzie complained. "You were a mere sheepherder's daughter, or as near as makes no difference, and I'm a member of the peerage. If anything, *you* owe *me*."

Her father owned hundreds of sheep and acres of land, not to mention the wool mills, but there had been no point in explaining the distinction to Adrian. He didn't care.

Cat hopped up. "There's the last scone gone. Come along, Lizzie. I have a trunk's worth of clothing to show you."

"A *trunk*! I thought you said a gown or two."

"Perhaps a few more," her sister said unrepentantly. "What's more, I brought back a French seamstress to make adjustments. You really ought to take her as a lady's maid. I can't imagine how you have survived without one."

Lizzie got up reluctantly. "The upstairs maid is good with buttons," she said, glancing down at her lavender morning gown, which was embellished with a long row of pearl buttons.

"Your gown was designed to be worn by a widow who lives with seven cats in a cottage in the country," Cat announced. "She is the vicar's right hand, reads novels from the Minerva Press in private and her prayer book in public, and carts around extra vegetable marrows from her garden, so everyone's heart sinks as soon as they see her."

Lizzie felt a little nauseated. She had been thinking of buying a cottage; she couldn't live in Adrian's house forever. But she didn't want to dwindle into a marrow-loving widow.

"Come along," Cat said coaxingly. "That partner of Joshua's, the one I told you about, hasn't married because he went to India and came back with a fortune from tea."

"I like a man who made his own fortune," Lizzie said cautiously. "Perhaps if he's been in India, and not in society, he won't know about Adrian."

"Of course, he's in society," her sister said, pulling her toward the door. "Do you think that I would match my sister with a merchant?"

"Papa was a merchant," Lizzie pointed out.

"Do you want your daughter labeled a 'Woolly Breeder'?"

"You'd prefer a 'Tempting Tealeaf'?" Lizzie said, smiling.

"That's more like you," Cat said, starting up the stairs. "You won't believe how lovely these gowns are, darling. Do come along!"

Chapter Seven

LIZZIE SPENT THE afternoon being poked and prodded by a French seamstress, which left plenty of time to think.

Bitterness was like a poison. Cat was right: She had to get rid of it. For the first time since Adrian died, she tried to imagine a future that included more than a blue bedroom and an endless supply of novels.

The problem was that every possible future she could think of included a man. She didn't want a man. But perhaps she wanted more than a stack of books.

When it was time to dress for dinner, she had two choices: she could wear her much-worn blue evening dress, or one of the Parisian gowns that her sister had bought for her.

The blue evening dress had been made years ago from excellent cloth. In the first year of her marriage, she had tried to take revenge by spending Adrian's money. But his estate had been entailed to a distant cousin, and it turned out that he didn't give a damn if she chalked up debts against the estate. He and Sadie were living on Lizzy's dowry.

It wasn't until she'd ordered an entire wardrobe suited to a lady that she discovered her husband had no plans to take her into society. He was ashamed of his marriage, ashamed of her.

"Why didn't you simply take a paid position, if you found the prospect of marrying a merchant's daughter so humiliating?" she had asked him.

"What?"

"Take a position as an estate manager or some such?"

Adrian had sighed. "Gentlemen don't *work*, Lizzie."

That was that.

In the end, she put on the old blue dress because she didn't want Mr. Berwick to think she was trying to entice him. Normally she wouldn't care, because she found it easy to ignore men.

Even in the few moments she'd talked to Mr. Berwick, she had found him impossible to ignore.

He was so big, for one thing. Tall, with broad shoulders, but that wasn't really it. He was beautiful, the way some Greek statues are beautiful, in an otherworldly type of way.

When she looked in the mirror, though, and saw the gown's unfashionably high waist, and the way it made her look as if she was trying to be girlish, she tore it off and donned one of the Parisian gowns.

The tiny bodice was boned to form its own corset and rather to Lizzie's surprise, it gave her a bosom whereas her old dresses made her look flat.

She wasn't dressing for Mr. Berwick, precisely. She was . . . she didn't know what she was doing.

The moment she walked into the drawing room, his eyes lit up and he began walking toward her. It gave her a distinct thrill to see that he was . . . well . . . interested. In her. She could see that in his eyes.

He moved toward her with the kind of whip-smooth movement that told her he was a rider, and probably a good one. His hair wasn't pomaded or arranged in any particular fashion; it tumbled around in thick curls.

She was late because of changing her dress, so Cat ushered everyone directly into the dining room. The girls were with them, and for some reason Cat launched into a lecture about how to manage suitors. True, both girls would debut the following spring, but Lizzie hated to think about it.

What if they didn't have any suitors? What if they found themselves at the side of the ballroom? All that instruction would go to waste.

She adored Cat, but her elder sister spent 80 percent of her time instructing someone about the right way to do things. Joshua was chiming in now, lending a gentlemen's perspective.

Mr. Berwick seemed to have as little to contribute on the subject as she did. It had been so long since Lizzie had conversed with someone other than a family member that she couldn't think of anything to say.

For his part, Mr. Berwick looked completely unperturbed at the silence between them. He had accepted an outrageous amount of beef pie and was eating it.

She hadn't the slightest inclination to eat supper, let alone something as heavy as that pie.

"How long have you been the guardian of your niece, Mr. Berwick?" she finally asked.

"Eleven months," he said. And then, without hesitation, "Why on earth did you marry Adrian Troutt?"

She blinked at him. "Those two questions are hardly commensurate."

"I don't see why not. You asked me about my family, and then I asked you about yours."

"Polite conversation is not a question game," she noted. "I do not consider Adrian a member of my family. He is my deceased spouse."

His eyes turned out to be indigo blue. There was a faint smile in them that made her stomach curl. "Don't you think men and women always play some sort of game while conversing?"

"I wouldn't know," Lizzie said, with perfect truth.

His brows drew together. "I wasn't in London when you debuted. So I truly don't know why you chose Adrian Troutt."

"I didn't choose him; my father did. He wanted my sister and me to be titled, and he was prepared to pay handsomely. Adrian presented himself, and Adrian had a title."

"Oh, right. Now I think of it, your sister said as much."

"Do you have family, Mr. Berwick?"

"I have a sister, Hattie's mother. She's in Egypt, ardently hoping that she can save souls by handing out cups of tea and reading the Bible aloud in a language people there don't understand. If she's not already in Africa, doing the same thing."

"Goodness," Lizzie said, a bit taken aback. "Sarah told me that Hattie's mother lived abroad."

"It sounds better that way, as if she might be taking waters in Switzerland, or on holiday in Portugal. Fortunately, Hattie and I have taken to each other, because her parents don't plan to return for years. You are not eating, Lady Troutt."

Lizzie look down at her plate. "I don't care for beef pie."

He glanced up and a footman instantly appeared at his side. "Take this away," he said. "Bring Lady Troutt something made from vegetables."

The footman bowed and departed.

"You needn't have done that," Lizzie remarked. She picked up her wine glass and fiddled with it.

"Why stare at food if you don't wish to eat it?" Clearly he liked beef, given the rate he was putting away his pie.

"I was taught to try each dish."

A footman slipped a plate in front of her. "Asparagus tart, my lady." It looked fresh and green, and far more appetizing than the brown sludge on Mr. Berwick's plate.

He watched her eat a bite and then nodded, which could have been patronizing but somehow wasn't.

"So your father forced you into marriage, and as a result you refuse to see him?" he asked.

Lizzie froze with her fork half way to her mouth. Then she took the bite, carefully chewed, and swallowed. "It seems you and my sister have had remarkably candid and wide-ranging conversations."

"Yes."

There was something intoxicating about the way Mr. Berwick's eyes focused on her face, the way he listened with complete concentration.

"I was not particularly angry about my father's choice of Lord Troutt," Lizzie said, surprising herself with the confession. "I only became angry after I fled my husband and my father refused to take me in."

Mr. Berwick made a grunting sign that somehow, improbably, Lizzie took as indicating support.

"If I ever have children," she added, "my home would always be open to them. *Always.*"

"Lucky children," he said.

Lizzie felt a flash of alarm. Mr. Berwick was dangerous, with his warm eyes and straightforward questions. He could make one believe that he had no secrets. That what you saw was . . . who he was. That he was honest in his dealings with the world.

What's more, the hint of desire in his eyes when he looked at her made her feel giddy, which was an absurd emotion.

"I don't mean to have any children, so it's a moot point," she told him, straightening her backbone, because she was showing an alarming tendency to lean toward him.

"Oh? Why not?" He didn't look critical, merely interested.

She ignored the obvious fact that she had no husband. "They look like howling plums, round and purple."

He gave a bark of laughter. "You're absolutely right. Howling plums wearing little white bonnets."

"Worst of all is when the plum has a huge shock of hair," she said, smiling despite herself. "What about you? Why aren't you married, with a fruit basket of your own, Mr. Berwick?" If he could be direct, so could she.

"I haven't fallen in love, and I see no point in marriage otherwise. I do not lack for company—for all my niece is convinced that I will wither from loneliness after she grows up."

Of course, he didn't lack for company. He likely had a Shady Sadie of his own, installed in a snug house, just as Adrian had.

That was the moment when she discovered that Mr. Berwick was able to anticipate her thoughts, as well as her love of vegetables.

"Not that sort of company," he said bluntly. "That wouldn't be appropriate, given that I am guardian to an impressionable young girl."

Lizzie discovered that she was smiling. "I expect that heartlessness is a useful attribute for a bachelor."

"Only if one wishes to remain unmarried."

His eyes caught hers, and an uneasy thrill went through her, as if someone had struck a gong just behind her shoulder. "Heartless conduct is definitely required of rakes," she said, striving for a careless tone. "I am a great reader of novels. In Lucibella Delicosa's books, rakish men are invariably ill-mannered."

Too late, she remembered the Wooly Breeder fiasco. "I didn't mean *that*!" she said. "You were very young."

"But definitely ill-mannered," he said wryly. "It was kind of your sister to overlook my conduct and invite me to her house, given our past."

"I suspect that you came all this way merely in order to apologize."

He nodded. "I did. But your sister turned something I had dreaded into a pleasure—and I would be glad I came even if that wasn't the case, because I've met you."

She could feel her cheeks turning pink, so she said hastily, "More people will arrive for the house party tomorrow."

"I'm not very good at small talk. Perhaps I will pretend to be your personal footman. I can make sure you are given something edible."

Lizzie looked down and realized with surprise that she'd eaten an entire slice of tart. A footman bowed and offered a serving of cod drowned in white sauce. Her stomach lurched at the smell of heavy cream and fish.

Mr. Berwick shook his head. "Lady Troutt doesn't want it," he told the footman. "Ask Bartleby to have the cook poach a small fillet and serve it with lemon."

She loved simple fish dishes, but it was a bit unnerving to find that Mr. Berwick guessed as much.

Lizzie drank some more wine. She couldn't complain, though he was awfully high-handed.

He didn't seem to feel the need to chatter, which was also nice.

"Did my sister inform you about who arrives tomorrow?" she asked.

"I gather Mr. Benjamin Jagger will join us." His face was noncommittal, but she had a distinct impression that he didn't approve. It was like being in a carriage and glimpsing a lake iced over: one could see the effect of the chill but not feel it.

"Why don't you like him?" she asked.

"I do like him." It seemed to be an honest answer. And yet . . .

She pursued her lips and was rather amused to see that his eyes followed the movement. He actually gave himself a little shake before he looked back at her eyes. Adrian had said her mouth was too large. In fact, he said several times that it was unfortunate, given his last name, that he married a woman with trout lips.

For some reason the memory didn't bother her this time.

"You do not like Mr. Jagger," she said. "I can tell by your face."

"Nonsense," Mr. Berwick said in a growly sort of voice. "Jagger is a solid fellow. I appreciate his good qualities. I just don't think he's appropriate company for ladies."

He took a bite of his fish. "You needn't worry. I will keep him away from you."

Lizzie liked his assumption that Mr. Jagger would pay her attention. "But has Cat told you all the guests who will arrive tomorrow?"

"No."

He sounded supremely uninterested.

Oh dear. Cat really ought to have warned him. "My sister's closest friend is the Countess of Mayne," Lizzie said. Then she waited.

His lips tightened. "That is a rather extraordinary co-incidence," he said, finally.

"I believe that the countess's sobriquet was the 'Scottish Sausage,'" Lizzie said, deciding that there was no point in obfuscating the subject.

He nodded silently.

"If it helps," she said, impulsively touching his right hand. "My sister truly wasn't distressed by the nickname she was given. She is a tremendously happy person, as you can see."

They both looked at Cat, shining at the top of the table, laughing at something her stepdaughter had said. "She's very good at being happy," Lizzie added. "When we were growing up, she often made Papa laugh by doing something frightfully silly. She used to keep a dormouse in her pocket and bring it out at dinner."

Mr. Berwick threw her a wary look. "Does she keep them around her person to this day? I have no particular fondness for rodents."

Lizzie grinned at him. "My brother-in-law knows just how to handle her. When she first showed Joshua her dormouse—who was named Sunflower—he went on and on about how the ancient Romans used to dip dormice in honey and poppy seeds and eat them for dessert."

When Mr. Berwick laughed, his eyes lightened to the color of an early morning sky. "Cooked or uncooked?" he inquired.

"I would assume cooked. According to Joshua, they also ate them at picnics. At any rate, when Cat married, she took the hint and gave Sunflower to our butler as a goodbye present."

"Was this a popular gift?"

"Absolutely. Sunflower came with a large fund for purchasing seeds and berries, and Joshua threw in two bottles of excellent brandy. So Sunflower lived a long and happy life in the butler's pantry—which was only a matter of another year or so."

"She was a lucky dormouse to find herself on sufferance in a butler's pantry."

"Indeed," Lizzie agreed. "I do think that Cat should have told you that Lord and Lady Mayne were among her guests. It would be rather shocking, I imagine, to come face-to-face without preparation."

Mr. Berwick shrugged. "I had intended to make my apologies to both ladies. It appears that fate has determined I do so expeditiously."

"I'm sure Cat told you how grateful she is that her first season went awry. If she hadn't been sent home in disgrace, she wouldn't have met delicious Joshua."

"'Delicious Joshua'?"

Lizzie nodded. "That's what she calls him." Her brother-in-law was leaning toward his wife, and as they watched, he dropped a kiss on her cheek. He wasn't nearly as good-looking as Mr. Berwick—but then, very few men were.

"I suppose if you like that beard," Mr. Berwick said, with the faintest touch of doubt in his voice.

She didn't, but she couldn't say so without making it sound as if she were flirting. Which she was not doing. "Would you like to practice your apology?" she asked.

"I beg your pardon?"

He really had the most marvelous way of *concentrating* on the person he was speaking to. It made Lizzie feel as if she might do something utterly silly, like burst into giggles. Or pull a dormouse out of her pocket to amuse him.

Lack of mice made the last option difficult, so she said, "Practice your apology. I could play the part of the sausage. I mean," she said hastily, "the Countess of Mayne."

"I couldn't possibly practice in public," Mr. Berwick said. He had a sort of severe elegance about him that kept tricking Lizzie into thinking he was falling into a bad humor.

But he wasn't. If she looked at his eyes, rather than at the patrician cast of his cheekbones and hard jaw, she discovered he was amused. In fact, he had an open face. And an open manner.

She had the idea that if he became angry, you'd know right away.

It was a much better way of living than bottling everything up inside because there was no way to inform Adrian of her feelings.

At the head of the table, Cat was standing, so Mr. Berwick brought Lizzie to her feet, tucked her arm under his elbow, and said, "I would be very grateful if you would allow me to rehearse my apology, Lady Troutt. Perhaps we can find a quiet corner in the drawing room."

Part of Lizzie—the quiet, contemplative part of her—thought this was a very bad idea. A different part of her thought that any reason to be alone with Mr. Berwick was a wonderful idea.

A fizzy, dizzyingly good idea, in fact.

Since the quiet part of Lizzie was never very good at speaking up, she gulped and allowed herself to be led into the drawing room.

Chapter Eight

So FAR, OLIVER had had little success making Cat's sister laugh. On the other hand, he hadn't unleashed any jokes—mostly because he couldn't remember any. He'd made a mental note to ask Hattie for a joke or two, but he had no faith that would do the trick.

At the moment, he was simply focused on not allowing Lizzie Troutt to escape and flee to her room.

He had the distinct impression that she wanted to go back to her reading and forget about him. She was unnerved. He could see it in her eyes but then . . . he could also see something else.

A confused but utterly delicious emotion. Hopefully, it was desire. Because, damn it, he was in the grip of a lust like nothing he'd felt before. It was making it hard to breathe.

And he was damned glad that his pantaloons were as generously cut as they were.

"Why don't we take a promenade?" he suggested, once they reached the drawing room. He squinted down to the end of the room. "We'll probably end up in the next county by walking far enough in that direction."

"For propriety's sake, we ought to remain with the others," Lizzie said. But she started walking.

She couldn't be worried about her reputation, given that the only people in the room were members of her family. "I promise not to make an untoward advance to you this evening," he said.

"I'm a widow, Mr. Berwick. I have no fears of that sort." And she turned up her little nose, as if being a widow meant no man would want her.

He wanted her, but he decided not to mention that he was definitely planning on making an untoward advance in the near future. They were reaching the shady end of the room.

"In the evening this room grows frightfully chilly and damp," Lady Troutt said. "We might take a chill."

She wanted to avoid him—a good instinct, because Oliver felt more and more like a fox who had stumbled on a particularly succulent chicken.

He wanted her.

He wanted to kiss the sadness out of her eyes, and ravish that wide mouth of hers until she looked as if she were wearing lip paint. He wanted to see her panting on his bed, all that glorious hair spilling around her shoulders. Maybe it fell all the way to her waist.

Lust went straight down his body in a shocking bolt of heat.

"Your gown is not intended to provide warmth," he said, unable to stop himself from glancing at her bosom. Gentlemen do not ogle a lady's breasts, even if her gown was so low that her breasts looked like presents, offered for his pleasure. Like creamy, silken—

He cut off that train of thought.

"This is a Parisian creation created from a few scraps of silk," Lizzie said disapprovingly. "I hate to think what my sister paid for it, given its lack of fabric."

"Surely you don't expect me to bemoan the fact that you aren't draped in bolts of cloth?" Oliver noted that his voice had dropped at least an octave.

Her mouth opened in a little circle. He leaned closer. "I was thinking of sending the modiste a personal thank you."

Rosy color swept into her cheeks.

This end of the drawing room was indeed rather chilly, with a distinct odor of damp. Oliver hated to cover up all that luscious skin, but he pulled off his coat and wrapped her in it.

"I cannot address you as Lady Troutt," he stated.

She was nestled in his coat, sunny hair scrunched against the collar. "Weren't you planning to address me as Lady Mayne?"

"For a few minutes, yes. But not thereafter." The words came out of his mouth without planning. "I dislike thinking of Adrian Troutt in connection with you."

"I wasn't aware that you knew my husband." Her eyes were cool and haunted again.

Damn it, she couldn't have loved that blighter, could she? Surely not.

"I knew of him. I spend almost all my time at my estate in Yorkshire and I rarely go into society."

"It would be most improper for you to address me as anything other than Lady Troutt," she observed.

"Yes, but here we are, without a chaperone. We're already being improper," he said, coming to the most extraordinary conclusion.

It seemed this was his girl.

His woman.

The person who would be his wife.

A slightly sad, utterly delectable woman named Lizzie Troutt.

They were far down the room, almost lost in the shadows. "Lizzie," he said.

She blinked at him with absurdly long eyelashes that made her look like an ostrich, large eyes surrounded by delicate fringes. "How do you know my first name? You mustn't address me so informally!"

Oliver had the idea that if he started kissing her, she might run from the room. He cleared his throat. "Are you ready to hear my apology?"

"There's no need to apologize," she said. "You can simply address me appropriately from now on and I'll—"

"Lizzie."

She stopped.

"I refuse to call you Lady Troutt because I don't want to think of you with that man. Not at all."

Her breathing seemed a little irregular. Was that a good sign? Silence stretched between them.

"So I shall call you Lizzie," he stated.

"All right," she said in a rush. "All right, you may address me as Lizzie but only here, that is, when no one can overhear us."

That would do for the moment.

"Are you prepared to pretend to be Lady Mayne?"

She gave herself a little shake, and raised her chin. "Yes, Mr. Berwick?" Her voice took on a faint but delightful Scottish burr.

"I apologize for calling you a sausage, whether it be Scottish, English, French . . . Portuguese."

"German sausages are also excellent," she offered. "But I don't think you should digress into particulars, Mr. Berwick."

"Oliver."

She hesitated, and then gave him a small smile. "This is monstrously improper. But all right, Oliver. I think you should concentrate on making your amends, rather than straying in a direction that might make the countess dwell too much on the roundness of sausages."

Oliver had no interest in countesses, and he couldn't pretend that he did. Lizzie had let his jacket fall open, which meant that the gentle curve of her breast gleamed like a hidden treasure.

He took a step closer. "I take one look at you, and I lose my mind and start thinking about food."

"Lord Mayne is unlikely to appreciate this approach. My sister tells me they are a most devoted couple."

He dragged his eyes away from the swell of her breasts. "I scarcely met you," he said, the words coming out rather raggedy, "before I knew that I wanted you."

"I think your apology needs more humility," Lizzie said, a smile trembling on her lips. She knew perfectly well that he was speaking of her, not the countess. "Perhaps you should get on your knees."

He saw shock in her eyes the moment the words left her mouth.

"I would get on my knees," he said carefully, "if you want me to."

"No," she gasped. "There's no need for that, Mr. Berwick, I mean, Oliver. I accept your apology. Truly. No word of sausages shall ever pass between us again."

"Very well," he said. "But you're certain that you don't wish me to apologize on my knees?"

"Absolutely certain!"

He took a final step, so that there was no air between their two bodies. "When I look at *you*, Lizzie, I don't think of sausages."

There was an aching tone in his voice that he'd never heard before from his own mouth, but he gave a mental shrug. For some reason, fate had put him here, with a beautiful woman who was staring up at him with an expression of utter confusion.

He wasn't confused. He was burning like a live coal.

He knew with a sudden, ferocious conviction that Lizzie had never been set alight at all. She was his, all his.

Never mind the fact she'd been married. She was still his.

"Looking at you, I think of peaches in the warm sunlight," he said, making another surprising discovery about himself. He had a poetic bent. "Silky, juicy peaches, the kind one cannot bear to eat and cannot bear not to eat."

Her eyes widened a bit. "Mr. Berwick—"

"Don't ever call me that again," he said with sudden violence. "My name is Oliver. It's actually Oliver John Berwick. I am a second son, but I inherited money from an aunt, and I have managed to turn that into a great deal more money. I am not a bad prospect for marriage."

Lizzie's mouth closed. "We have digressed," she said with a gulp. "The Countess of Mayne will not have the faintest interest in marrying you; by all accounts, she is very much in love with her husband, and divorce is difficult to obtain in England."

"Yes, isn't it a good thing that I didn't meet you before Troutt died?" Oliver said, adding, "I might have had to kill him."

"Kill him?" Oliver's future wife squealed. "What on earth are you talking about, Mr.—" She stopped, catching the look in his eye. "Oliver."

"Say it again."

"What—"

Oliver succumbed to temptation and pulled her into his arms. "Say my name again."

"We shouldn't do this," she breathed.

He looked down at her. "We should."

"*Oliver*," she said, frowning at him. "I can see that you are—you are—well, I'm not sure what you're doing."

"Planning to marry you."

"Absolutely not!"

"Seduce you?"

She looked rather horrified, which made Oliver grin. "May I kiss you?"

"No! I think you have lost your mind."

"That is quite possible." She had the most delightful, straight nose he had ever seen. They would have beautiful offspring, as long as the poor scraps inherited her nose, not his. "Do you truly loathe the idea of children?"

"This conversation has gone far enough," she said, pulling out of his arms and trotting off toward the other side of the room as if the furies were at her shoulder.

Oliver followed her, thinking hard.

He'd never had any faith in fate, but he was obviously wrong.

Fate had put both women he'd wronged in his life in the same house, together with the woman he was meant to marry.

And have children with. Or not.

He didn't really care.

The only thing he cared about was making certain that Lizzie Troutt was his, within the day, if possible, but definitely before Benjamin Jagger darkened the door of Telford Manor.

Chapter Nine

LIZZIE LAY AWAKE a long time that night, staring at the ceiling. Oliver Berwick had flirted with her. No man had ever flirted with her before this evening, but she had no trouble recognizing it.

What's more, she was fairly certain that he meant to seduce her. For one thing, he told her that he meant to.

And for another, he compared her to a peach.

She spent a certain amount of time feeling happily peachlike. Still, she truly didn't want to be in Oliver's fruit basket, even if he had laughed at her joke about babies and plums.

Hopefully, he wouldn't repeat her comment to her sister, because Cat might take offense at the idea that her baby boys had resembled plums.

They looked better now, of course. At four and five, her nephews had fairly intelligent faces, and asked interesting questions. Yesterday she'd had a long conversation with the future Lord Windingham about whether people would recognize each other in heaven.

"Mama said that your husband died," he had said, in that straightforward way that children had. "But you won't die for years. When you get up there, you'll probably have white hair and a cane and all that sort of thing. How will he possibly know who you are?"

"It's quite possible that Lord Troutt won't recognize me," she had said, feeling quite happy about that prospect.

"But I want Mama to know who I am!" His bottom lip began wobbling.

"Your mother will always recognize *you*, because she's your mother. And you will recognize her."

"That's true," he had said, looking relieved. "Do you think there is an ant heaven, and do you think that mother ants recognize their babies? And what about the bad place?"

Lizzie had frowned, so he had said a bit impatiently, "The place you go if you don't go to heaven. Do you think when ants get into the butter, the way they did yesterday, they go to a bad place?"

Lizzie may not have liked Adrian very much, but she didn't want him to be in a bad place, so she said a hasty prayer for his soul.

Now, in bed, she started wondering how she felt about endangering her own soul by allowing herself to be seduced.

She finally decided that she wasn't too worried about heaven. She had attended church regularly with her mother, and thereafter with Adrian's mother. Left to her own devices, she would rather not listen to yet another man dictate what kind of woman she was supposed to be, no matter whether he was wearing black robes or no.

That didn't mean that she was ready to embark on an *affaire* that would turn her into Shady Sadie, either.

In fact, the more she thought about it, the more dubious the idea seemed to be. For one thing, Mr. Berwick had told her that he wasn't enjoying female company because he had an impressionable young niece.

Yet he immediately tried to seduce her in the drawing room, with two young girls not far away. Either he was fibbing about not having a mistress, or he was recklessly imprudent.

Either way, she would do well to avoid him.

At the same time, she had to admit that there was something about Oliver Berwick's blue eyes and broad chest that she found alluring.

Alluring wasn't a strong enough word.

When he looked at her intently, she began thinking inappropriate things about what it would feel like to touch him. Or if he touched her.

She was absolutely certain that if she ever saw him naked, she wouldn't feel the instinctive revulsion that she felt on first sight of Adrian's unclothed body.

And she was also pretty sure that Oliver's private part, for want of a better word, wouldn't look like a white snail without its shell, curled and soft.

As her husband's had.

The very thought of that proved a shock to the system.

Oliver Berwick was not good for her. He made her consider improper subjects.

It was one thing to decide that she wouldn't marry again. It was another to contemplate an illicit rendezvous with a man so practiced in his approaches and compliments.

Having made up her mind, she finally went to sleep. In an effort to avoid temptation, she kept to her room through breakfast and luncheon the following day.

But for the first time in her recent memory, she didn't feel peaceful, even though she was tucked away with an excellent novel to read.

Instead, she kept putting her book down and puttering around the room. She even looked through her Parisian gowns and chose one to wear in the evening.

Rather surprisingly, her sister didn't try to coax her out. Every once in a while she heard the noises of maids, but the big house was oddly silent.

It made her feel, fancifully enough, like Cat's dormouse, confined to the butler's pantry and left behind when her mistress pranced off to married life.

Late in the afternoon, she heard laughter and found herself tossing aside her book and running to her window.

Tramping across the grass, looking messed and rather sunburned, came Mr. Berwick with his niece Hattie and her step-niece Sarah. He was carrying a pail, and it looked to Lizzie as if they'd been fishing.

She loved fishing.

Correction: she used to love fishing. Adrian would never have approved; shooting was the only such activity he deemed not *labor*. Labor was not for Adrian, nor for any gentleman.

Oliver didn't seem to have learned that rule.

As she watched, he threw back his head and laughed. His throat was a strong, brown column, so attractive that she wrapped her arms around herself tightly, as if she could hold in the odd, explosive feelings in her stomach.

She meant to have nothing to do with him, with men in general . . . had she forgotten that? She turned back to her book.

She was sitting in a chair reading industriously, when her sister burst into the room.

"Lizzie," Cat said, without further greeting, "you must come downstairs to supper." Her sister dropped into a chair and scowled at her. "I'm tired of finding you in this room. I want you to go back to being yourself."

"I *am* myself," Lizzie pointed out. "I couldn't stay a girl forever, Cat. You still think of me as a five-year-old girl running about in a pinafore. I'm a grown woman."

Cat sighed. "I know you are. I just don't want you to be such a cowardly grown woman."

Lizzie's back straightened. "I'm not!"

"Yes, you are. You took one look at Oliver Berwick, and you ran to your room like a timid rabbit and stayed here all yesterday and today. I don't believe for a moment that you have a headache."

"I don't have a headache," Lizzie admitted. "I just find my book very interesting."

Her sister leaned sideways so she could see the book

cover. "You're still reading *The Betrothed*. I forgot most of it, but it was set in the 1100s and deadly boring. Don't try to tell me it's interesting. I know better."

Lizzie closed the book. "You were never much good at reading, Cat."

"All I remember is the heroine being forced to stay in a haunted bedchamber. Sir Walter Scott should have thought up something better than that. I'm sick of ghosts rattling their chains."

"Don't tell me! I haven't reached that yet."

"I'll leave you to your medieval ghosts, but only if you come down for dinner. I promised the girls that we could have a game of croquet in the drawing room."

"When you played it at Christmas, didn't your husband put a ball straight through the wall?"

"The hole's been patched," Cat said cheerfully. "We have new hoops, and the housekeeper has already taken up the rug. It needed to be beaten before the party arrives tomorrow anyway."

"I don't think that you're supposed to be pounding hoops into a drawing room floor," Lizzie said. But she couldn't help smiling. Her sister was such a madcap kind of person.

"That's better!" Cat said. "I shall leave you to that unpleasant ghost. I still remember the prophecy about the heroine."

"A prophecy! Don't tell me!" Lizzie exclaimed. But then she caught her sister's sleeve. "No, tell me. Otherwise I won't come to dinner because I'll be trying to read to that point."

Cat stuck out her hip and flung her left hand into the air.

"Is that the way the ghost looked?" Lizzie inquired.

"I could be on the stage," Cat told her. "If Joshua ever loses all his money and we have to sell this pile of stone, I'll play Lady Macbeth in order to keep food on the table."

"Never mind that, just play the ghost for the moment," Lizzie ordered.

"*Widowed wife, and married maid,*" Cat declaimed. "*Betrothed, betrayer, and betrayed.*"

Lizzie looked back at her book. "I'm starting to feel sorry for Eveline. I didn't realize she was going to be betrayed. I can see the 'widowed wife.' But 'married maid'?"

"Her marriage wasn't consummated," Cat said promptly. "At least I think that's the case but to be honest, I didn't like Eveline. I started skipping pages after she was told to remain safely in a castle, but instead she went out in the woods, where she was seized by rebels, *of course!*"

"I could be Eveline," Lizzie said, rather startled. "I'm a 'widowed wife.'"

"And a 'married maid'," Cat added.

Lizzie shrugged and looked down at her book. "I've been betrothed and betrayed, but I haven't been a betrayer."

"You should have," Cat said darkly. "You should have had a flagrant *affaire* that everyone knew about. You should have given birth to a son who would have inherited Adrian's estate, and he would have known that it wasn't his and there would have been nothing he could do about it!"

"It's too late for that."

"True. I do wish you'd been at luncheon, Lizzie. I'm becoming fast friends with Oliver Berwick. He's frightfully passionate about steam engines and I think he talked my husband into investing in a railway, which would be a good thing since this house takes a ferocious amount of money to keep up. Something is always falling apart."

"Perhaps if you didn't play croquet in the house, it wouldn't need so many repairs," Lizzie suggested.

"We have bigger problems, like the roof. Wear that pale yellow gown with that wonderful black and yellow sash tonight."

"It makes me feel like a French bumblebee," Lizzie said.

"It makes you look divine," Cat said. "Only the French would figure out how to make a woman's waist look so tiny. I love the way the hem is weighted to make it swirl at the bottom. It's just the thing for leaning over and hitting a croquet ball."

"Have you changed your mind about matchmaking and Mr. Berwick?" Lizzie asked suspiciously.

"Absolutely not," Cat said. "You'd never get along. He's far too clever for comfort."

Too clever? What man was too clever?

In Lizzie's experience, men did a reliable job of pretending to be clever, but it generally fell apart because they were such emotional creatures.

Take their father, for example. He was always trying to calculate odds, but in the end, he just bumbled along like anyone else.

Suddenly she remembered a day when he had brought her to see a whole pen full of baby lambs. She had squealed and shrieked with excitement—she couldn't have been more than six—and he let her climb into the pen and pet them for a long time, even though they lipped her hair and her bootlaces.

Her father hadn't always been focused on turning her into Lady Troutt. Not back then, when she was his Lizzie, and he was only her Papa.

Chapter Ten

Oliver was rather annoyed when Lizzie didn't appear for breakfast and lunch. She didn't eat enough, and avoiding meals wasn't a good idea. He'd had enough trays brought to his bedchamber to know that the cook would have sent up a finicky plate with barely enough food for an invalid.

He was falling short as a knight errant. He only had one more day to get her on a horse, not to mention in a fit of hilarity. Thinking about that, he walked into the drawing room and found it empty but for Sarah and his niece.

Hattie bounded to her feet, dragging Sarah with her. "Here's my best-of-uncles," she cried. "Please, may we go fishing again tomorrow?"

"Perhaps," Oliver said vaguely. If Lizzie didn't come to dinner, he might have to take matters into his own hands and root her out of her bedchamber. He had a shrewd idea he'd moved too quickly the night before.

No woman wants a man she's just met to drop to his knees. She wants to be wooed.

"I enjoyed fishing very much, Mr. Berwick," Sarah said, dropping a shy curtsy. She'd probably do very well in her debut; she was sweet, quite pretty, and exquisitely dressed, which hinted at a substantial dowry.

Then he frowned. His niece was equally well dressed.

Hattie caught his eye and looked down at her evening dress. "Isn't this beautiful? Sarah let me wear it."

"I hope you don't mind," Sarah said somewhat anxiously. "I have far more clothes than I can use and that color makes me quite sallow."

A footman handed Oliver a glass of wine. "Why on earth did you acquire a gown in an unacceptable color?" he inquired.

"My stepmother liked this figured silk," Sarah said with a little smile, "and I wanted to make her happy."

Hattie slung her arm around Sarah's neck and gave her a smacking kiss on the cheek. "You are the nicest girl in the world." Then she turned back to Oliver, her eyes shining. "Isn't this the most wonderful party you've ever been to?"

Oliver rather agreed with her, so he nodded.

"Did you hear that we're going to play croquet after the meal?" she cried.

"It's already dark outside," Oliver pointed out.

"We play in the drawing room," Sarah explained.

Bartleby opened the door. Oliver glanced over and froze, his wine glass halfway to his mouth.

Lizzie was wearing a gown that made her look like a

streak of sunshine or a lemon tart, something so dainty and delectable that a man licked his lips just to see her. He could have spanned her waist with his hands, but then he realized that her hips swelled to a lovely curve, and he wanted his hands there instead, sliding around her, pulling her body against his.

Bloody hell.

"Lady Troutt," he said, heading straight toward her like a ship navigating by the North Star. Even if he couldn't pull her into his arms, he could kiss her hand. "Good evening. I trust you had a restful day?"

Hattie and Sarah were trotting along behind him. "You missed fishing," Hattie said, bobbing a curtsy.

"It was absolutely fizzing!" Sarah cried.

"Good evening, Mr. Berwick," Lizzie murmured, not meeting his eyes. "Girls, how are you both?"

"We are fine, Aunt Lizzie," Sarah chirped. "Are you ready for to play croquet?"

"Absolutely," she said. The footman offered her a glass of wine, but she shook her head and turned to the girls, shifting so that Oliver was excluded from the conversation.

Not only did she avoid him in the drawing room by using the girls as deftly as a brick wall, but she managed to seat herself at the other end of the table.

Over dinner, Oliver watched as she took a small nibble of ham, refused to consider blood sausage, and pushed a piece of game pie around her plate.

Who could laugh when she had nothing to eat?

He called over the butler and had a brief talk with

him. Then he watched as Bartleby offered Lizzie something that looked a fricassee of wild greens, likely meant to be a side dish. She carefully removed the bacon sprinkled on top and ate the rest.

So she didn't like meat.

When they moved on to a course of roast goose, Bartleby offered Lizzie what seemed to be an orange-colored soup. Carrot bisque, perhaps?

To Oliver's satisfaction, a while later she ate every bite of an artichoke tart.

She gave him a slightly suspicious look. He'd never seen anything as beautiful as the particular hazel color of her eyes.

"Good evening," he said softly, ignoring the rule that dictated he speak only to Sarah, on his left, or Cat, on his right.

Lizzie gave him a dismissive smile and turned back to Hattie.

She probably rarely felt hungry because she stayed in her room too much. That would also explain why her skin was such an exquisite pale cream color.

She had turned her shoulder to him, so he felt free to stare at her while he ate. She had high cheekbones, and a little shell of an ear. She kept smiling faintly at things Hattie and Sarah came up with. They were listing all the socially unacceptable things they intended to do after they were married, such as travel in the mail coach, and ride a velocipede.

There was something about her tight smile that didn't feel right. Lizzie had the same generous bottom lip that

Cat had. A man took one look at that mouth and wanted to do—

Well.

All those things.

Her mouth was made for laughing.

What an idiot Adrian Troutt had been, living with someone named Shady Sadie when he could have been going home to his wife.

Lizzie smiled once again, and Oliver decided she might have dimples, if she laughed. It was a possibility.

By the end of the meal, he had come up with a plan. When Cat began herding everyone toward the drawing room, Lizzie looked anywhere but at him, so he didn't bound forward and take her arm, as he wished to.

He had to handle this carefully, so he silently followed her, appreciating the view. She had so much hair that it looked like a yellow puff pastry, hovering in the air above her slender neck. Her waist was nipped in and her skirt swelled out, the way skirts did these days. He liked the way it emphasized her curves.

He liked curves. Not overly lush curves, but ones like Lizzie's.

In fact, he liked everything about Lizzie Troutt except her last name.

Cat bounded up and took his arm, forcing him to stop ogling her sister. "Where did your husband go?" he inquired. Joshua had disappeared before Bartleby served tea.

"He's setting up the croquet game."

"I've never actually played, though I have a general

understanding of the game. I wouldn't have thought it could be played indoors; what do we do for hoops?"

"You'll see," Cat said.

Sure enough, when they walked into the drawing room, it had been transformed. The rugs were up, and hoops had been driven straight into the wide wood flooring.

Joshua was directing footmen in the art of placing chairs where they would cause the greatest impediment to putting a ball through the hoops. Cat instantly deserted him, flying toward her husband.

"No, no!" she cried. "That chair has to be at right angles to the hoop." A footman obediently shifted an ancient chair with magnificent lion paws for legs, probably dating back to the reign of King Henry VIII.

Sarah trotted up and handed Oliver a crimson mallet, and her father a green one. Joshua swished it through the air so Oliver swung his as well.

"I gather you've never played croquet," Joshua said.

Oliver shook his head.

"You'll want to turn it about and hit the ball with the other end."

Oliver flipped the mallet over. "It's just a matter of hitting balls through hoops, right?"

"Pretty much. Want to place a bet on the outcome?"

"Have I told you that I'm a champion billiards player?"

Joshua snorted. "Billiards is old-fashioned. Croquet is the new billiards."

"Gentlemen!" Cat shouted. "If you could please stop nattering, we are ready to begin the game."

Oliver positioned himself beside Lizzie. She moved away, and he followed. "I've never played," he said apologetically, "so I need to watch your stroke."

"My stroke?"

She had delicate brows, but they took on quite a fierce look when she drew them together.

"How you handle your mallet," he explained.

The girls were having an argument over who got the prettiest croquet mallet—which turned out to be the purple one.

"Didn't I understand that you're such a good billiards player that croquet will be child's play for you?" she asked.

Apparently she had been eavesdropping.

He grinned. "You have no faith in my skills?"

"Croquet is a child's game," Lizzie said, slumping back into cool disdain again. "I'm sure you can win if you feel that passionately about it, Mr. Berwick."

"*Oliver,*" he said.

She raised an eyebrow. "We are not alone."

"No one is paying the slightest attention. I don't suppose you'd like to place a wager on which of us ends up with the better score?"

He saw a flicker deep in her eyes. Cat was right; Lizzie was competitive as hell.

"I wouldn't have thought you'd display such ill breeding as to play for money in front of your niece," she said loftily.

Oliver would love to kiss that look right off her face. He'd love to plunge into her plush lips and kiss her until there was nothing bored or disdainful in her face. Until she had red cheeks and glazed eyes, and was gasping his name.

He had lost track of the conversation, and she was staring at him.

"I didn't mean a bet for money," he said hastily. "Merely a wager. The prize to be something you want."

For a moment he had her, and then a veil slipped back over her eyes. "There's nothing I want," she said politely. "But I do wish you the best of luck. I'm quite certain you will win. I haven't played croquet in years."

Not since she married, then.

"In that case, we are evenly matched," he said coaxingly.

"A wager would be most inappropriate."

"If I win, you'll go for a ride with me tomorrow morning," he stated.

Her face turned a little pink. "You are so persistent!"

"Yes, it's one of my best characteristics," he acknowledged, holding her gaze. "When I see something I want, I go after it."

She bit her lip during the silence that followed this statement.

"I want to go for a ride tomorrow morning," Oliver said, finally.

Her eyes shifted to the girls, who were still squabbling over the purple mallet.

"I can't get Hattie out of bed before late morning," he said, "and what's more, I am deaf from high-pitched squealing that came from threading worms onto fishing hooks earlier today. I'm desperate for adult company."

"Why don't you go for a ride alone?" she asked.

"I don't know the area," he said promptly.

"Neither do I!"

"The truth is that I don't want to be lonely. I don't like riding by myself. I'm a sociable creature."

It was a shameless lie, and he held his breath, waiting for her to answer.

"*If* you win, I shall accompany you," she said finally. "But there will be no badgering me if you lose."

"I shan't lose," he said carelessly.

Sure enough, something kindled in her eyes at his statement. He grinned at her. "Will you tell me the rules?"

"I can't believe you think you'll win the game without ever having played before!"

"I have an excellent reason to win," he said, pitching his voice low and for her ears only.

"We need to form teams, because we have more than four players," Joshua called. "Everybody come down to this end."

The girls quickly formed a team, which saved the purple mallet from being cracked in two. They huddled together with a ferocious look in their eyes that suggested—from Oliver's knowledge of his niece—that they fully intended to win by hook or by crook. Or, in layman's terms, by cheating.

"I'll partner my wife," Joshua said. "We'll go in order of oldest to youngest."

"No, no, youngest to oldest," Hattie shouted, dancing on one leg.

Oliver thought about whether he should tell her to

calm down, but he wasn't her parent, nor her governess. Not that she had a governess. His sister had kept Hattie at school until the day before she dropped her daughter at his house.

That meant he was *in loco parentis*.

"Hattie, settle down," he said.

She rolled her eyes and said, somewhat more quietly, "I'm the youngest and my uncle is the oldest, so I claim the right to go first."

It took Oliver a few minutes to figure out the game. There were hoops—he'd known that—and colored mallets and balls painted to match. But there were also chairs strewn around the room, which made things more difficult.

Everything progressed more or less civilly, until he began to win. At that point Joshua started gripping his mallet harder than necessary—which threw off his aim, as Oliver took some pleasure in pointing out.

Lizzie got a squinty-eyed look that he discovered he liked far better than placidity, and began hitting the ball harder. Faster.

More erratically.

Clearly, she needed some tutoring.

After her ball went awry once again and slammed into the wall, knocking out a chunk of plaster, he stepped up behind her and before she could say a word, put his arms around her waist and his hands over hers. "Look down."

"Mr. Berwick!" she hissed. "Stand back."

"I'm doing you a service. You've got no aim whatsoever." She smelled delectable and mysterious.

"I do! This is most improper."

"Nonsense," he said, deliberately making his tone impatient. "Look at your sister."

Joshua had Cat wrapped in his arms, supposedly so he could direct her croquet mallet, but Oliver didn't think they were concentrating on the game very much. For one thing, they were at least five strokes behind.

"This is the only way to tutor a player in the correct posture," Oliver said. "Look down and put the ball directly in front of you. *Then* swing the mallet."

He heard Lizzie's breath catch as he moved his body into full contact with hers, though likely she wasn't experiencing the monstrous wave of lust that he felt. He hadn't held a woman in his arms in months, not since before Hattie became part of his household.

He had already had a cockstand, but now he had become painfully stiff.

Lizzie was worrying her lush lower lip with small white teeth, which just made things worse.

"That's better," he said, as she positioned herself directly above the ball. "Do you see the leg of that chair? If you aim at the right front chair leg, the ball will rebound from the chair and go through the hoop. The leg is at just the right angle."

She leaned over peering at the hoop, which meant she pushed back against his body. Oliver stifled a groan because he was fairly sure she didn't mean to press her delectable rear end against him.

Lizzie seemed oblivious to what was happening to his body—though she had to feel his tool against her rear.

He still had his arms around her, and his hands loosely positioned over hers.

"Right," she said, swinging the mallet and hitting the ball with a solid *thunk*.

It rolled forward, struck the leg, and rebounded straight through the hoop. For a moment they both stared silently.

Then Lizzie gave a yelp, broke from his arms, and screamed, "I did it!"

Oliver fell back a step. The pale widow was gone. Her cheeks were pink and her eyes were shining.

"Hurrah!" her sister cried, hurrying over. "Oh, I set up that hoop. Wasn't it clever? You have to bounce it off a chair leg or it's impossible."

"Yes, and just look what's happened to the chair," her husband said, joining them. "I think that belonged to my great-grandfather."

"It will survive the game," Cat said, obviously unperturbed. She flashed a look of deep approval at Oliver and then turned back to her sister. "I saw Mr. Berwick coaching you. That's not fair."

"You have a coach, and I can hardly help it if you and Joshua are far behind," Lizzie retorted, a distinct note of glee in her voice.

"We were only one stroke behind you," Cat said. "That was a lucky shot. I've always been better than you at outdoor games."

"No, you're haven't," Lizzie protested. "Only at badminton."

Cat laughed. "I love the way my baby sister always tries to keep up with me."

Lizzie drew in a sharp breath. Oliver had fully intended to win the bet, but all of a sudden he changed his mind.

Fire had flared in Lizzie's eyes at her elder sister's challenge. Cat was deliberately needling her, trying to bring out her competitive side.

Oliver had the feeling it had worked. And he wanted Lizzie to win.

Cat had turned away and was lining up her next shot. With a wicked grin, Joshua wrapped himself around his wife again. Oliver understood precisely why Joshua didn't mind sacrificing the drawing room furniture to play croquet with his family.

He turned back to Lizzie. She was chewing her lip again and eyeing the next hoop, which was hammered in at a diagonal. "If I can make it so that you beat your sister, will you go riding with me?" he asked.

Her eyes sparkled. "Yes!"

"Right." He raised his voice. "I'm going to drop out and devote myself to coaching Lady Troutt."

"Coaching!" Cat scoffed, turning her head. "I thought you didn't know how to play, Oliver."

"I don't," he said innocently. "So no one can have the faintest objection if I put my own mallet to the side." Without further ado, he wrapped himself around Lizzie, loving the moment when her soft body relaxed into his.

She smelled intoxicatingly good.

"The only way to make this hoop is by a long shot," he said, eyeing the course while they waited for the girls to finish their turn. "We're going to have to skim the table leg just enough to change the direction of the ball, then slice it under that chair and through the hoop. We need a thirty-degree angle."

Lizzie turned inside his embrace. "Oliver, that's impossible," she said urgently.

He smiled down at her, knowing that his face had to be plainly desirous and not giving a damn. She'd been a married woman. She would know desire when she saw it.

Her eyelashes fluttered and she lowered her eyes, her cheeks staining a beautiful raspberry.

"We can do it," he said, realizing that his voice had gone husky. Hattie finished her turn with a loud whoop.

Lizzie seemed to have lost her courage. "Perhaps I should just try on my own."

"You are going to let your sister beat you?" Oliver said, raising an eyebrow. The answer was in her face, so he spun her about and tucked her close to his body again. "Ball directly below us, now position the mallet just right so that it will strike off the table leg . . ."

They didn't get the precise angle he wanted, but close enough.

"We didn't make it," Lizzie said, with disappointment.

Oliver just barely stopped himself from dropping a kiss on her nose. "We're only one stroke away. No one else has made it through that hoop in less than four turns."

The smile spreading through her eyes was wonderful.

And her utterly sensual mouth was curved in a genuine smile.

Someone tapped him on his shoulder, and he turned his head. Cat was standing beside him, a curious look in her eyes.

"Oh, Oliver!" she cooed.

Lizzie had moved away and she was bending over, investigating where the ball had come to rest.

"I've got her smiling," he said wrenching his eyes away from Lizzie's magnificent rear end. "Very close to a laugh."

"Excellent job," Cat whispered. "I was going to remind you of your quest, but I see you have it well in hand."

"Make Lizzie laugh," Oliver said obediently. "Get her out of doors. She's promised to ride with me tomorrow morning."

"With a groom, I hope," Cat said.

"Of course." Not that he had any intention of taking a chaperone.

Benjamin Jagger was arriving tomorrow. Ben was far more interested in railways than anything else. He would never play croquet with a couple of schoolgirls, and certainly not in a drawing room.

To be fair, Oliver didn't know anyone who played croquet in the drawing room.

But once Ben saw Lizzie, he would forget about railroads.

"You saw her smile, didn't you?" Oliver asked. "I'm almost there."

Cat nodded. "I saw yours as well." She gave him a pat on the shoulder. "Just don't tempt me to use this mallet on your head rather than the ball, hmmm?"

"Of course not," Oliver said.

He had just been struck—not by a mallet, but by a thought.

The Wooly Breeder business had been a cloud over his head, whether he realized it or not. Not only was it gone, but Cat had become a friend, for all she had her eyes narrowed as if she could shoot a few holes in him with mere willpower.

It felt as if the lifted weight left room inside him for something else. Something surprising.

Shocking, even.

Lizzie was crouched down, tipping her head to the side so she could visualize the possible path of the ball, just as he had taught her. She looked over her shoulder and caught him staring.

"I don't think we can do it," she said, not noticing what was in his eyes. She seemed to be a very not-noticing type of woman. Either that, or Troutt was a bigger idiot than he would have thought.

"Yes, we can," he said, clearing his throat.

He dropped down beside her on the floor and pointed out exactly how they were going to stroke the ball, so gently that it would go through the hoop as sweetly as—

He broke off.

Lizzie was looking at him intently, and a shiver went down his back from the pure erotic force of being this close to her.

The two of them were crouched down behind the wooden back of an old-fashioned settee, out of sight. No one was paying them any attention; the other players had erupted into a quarrel about whether Hattie had cheated.

His niece had cheated; he was certain of it.

"Yes?" Lizzie prompted.

How could she have that buttercup hair with darker eyebrows? And how could she have that mouth without every man in the vicinity wanting to kiss her?

By every man, he meant Benjamin Jagger.

And himself.

There was only one answer.

Oliver leaned forward and brushed his lips over hers. She started, but when she didn't topple over backward trying to get away, he reached out and took her delicate shoulders in his hands, and kissed her again.

She let out her breath in a startled puff of air, so he took advantage and slipped his tongue inside her mouth.

She started again, for all the world as if she'd never been kissed. He didn't waste time wondering about it; he slid his fingers into her hair, tipped her head just so, and kissed her deeply.

He probably only had a minute before someone wondered where they were. Consequently, the kiss was fast, and hard, and slightly mad.

Intoxicating.

Chapter Eleven

AFTER OLIVER KISSED her behind the settee, Lizzie lost interest in the game. But Oliver didn't. There was no question but that he was ferociously competitive. He had dropped out of the game, and if he wasn't going to win, she was.

Obviously, winning wasn't his only goal.

He kept putting his arms around her, telling her that she was holding the mallet incorrectly. Every time their eyes met, it sent a thrill down her spine because the look in his eyes . . .

Adrian had been nearly as round as he was tall. But Oliver's body was hard and muscled, his stomach flat. When he put his arms around her, she felt protected, which made her realize that she hadn't felt safe since the moment her father walked her to the altar and left her there.

She had felt safe as a child. She and her friends at

school had spent their free time reading novels and pining for the music master, who hadn't the faintest interest in any of them.

She'd always known that she would have no hand in choosing her husband. That was the way of it, when you were a merchant's daughter—albeit a remarkably rich merchant's daughter—whose father intended that his daughters would marry into the peerage.

Men would bid on her, and the highest bidder would win. When it became clear that Adrian Troutt was determined to win her hand, she had resigned herself to the fact.

Adrian had a nice twinkle in his eye, and she could have done worse. She had been a good girl, blindly certain that if she behaved obediently, she and her husband would come to love each other.

Even if they didn't, she would have children to think about.

A hand touched her cheek, a passing caress. "What's the matter?" Oliver asked.

"You shouldn't touch me like that!" she managed, every thought of Adrian flying from her mind. Every time she looked at Oliver, she couldn't breathe.

"I like touching you," he said in a low voice.

"Oliver!"

His smile was pure wicked delight, spurring the irrepressible thought that Lizzie didn't have to *marry* a man in order to enjoy him. She was a widow, after all. There were all those ballads about lusty widows.

She could be one of those. A loose woman.

Heat surged up her neck and into her cheeks. His kisses . . . She hadn't known that kisses could be so intimate. She would like more of those kisses.

Oliver's eyes went heavy lidded, which meant he guessed what she was thinking about. His hand slid off the croquet mallet and onto her bare arm.

"Did you know," he asked, in that deep voice of his, "that it's possible to play croquet in a bedchamber as well as a drawing room?"

She *never* giggled, but one flew from her lips. "Cat came up with the idea of indoor croquet. She's never mentioned the bedchamber."

"You could play the game anywhere." He drew closer, his body warming hers, his fingers drifting up the skin of her arm. "All you need is a mallet and a hoop."

Lizzie felt her eyes go wide. Oliver's front was plastered against her back, and she suddenly realized that he definitely didn't share Adrian's problem. His mallet . . . well.

"You're driving me mad," he said in rough whisper.

She twisted her head to see his face. She'd never seen desire like that, not for her, and it was heady stuff. It made her feel as if she'd drunk far too much wine. It was a fizzy feeling, like . . . like happiness.

"It's your turn, Lizzie," Cat called. "If you and Oliver would please pay attention to the game, we could finish this before midnight!"

"We are coming," Oliver called, his voice as smooth as could be. Then he said, "Do you still refuse to marry me?"

"What?" Lizzie squealed.

"If you remember, I as good as asked you yesterday. I was hoping you'd changed your mind."

"I don't wish to marry anyone," she said firmly. He was teasing. He had to be teasing.

"Would you mind being seduced by me?"

"Mind? Of course I'd mind!"

He moved so quickly that she couldn't stop him. He turned his back so she was shielded from the other players and then kissed her hard so that longing rose in her stomach like a storm, making her knees weak and her breath fast. He didn't stop until she was boneless, leaning against him like a hussy.

"I would not mind being seduced by you," Oliver stated, his voice as dark and soft as velvet. "But my preference would be to marry you as well."

He was a truth-teller, she realized. He said what he was thinking, no matter how scandalous or improper.

She looked up, steadying herself with hands on his chest. There was a mixture of arrogance and burning longing in his eyes that she instinctively responded to.

"Do you consider me a woman of—of ill repute?" she whispered. She meant to scold him by the question, but it came out a simple inquiry.

"Absolutely not."

"You wouldn't tell anyone?"

"A gentleman never tells." Oliver said that fiercely.

"I'm sorry," she said. "I didn't mean to insult you." *Adrian* always told. Adrian had told the whole kingdom that he adored Sadie Sprinkle.

His eyes searched hers and he answered the questions she couldn't put in words. "I don't have a mistress. I haven't slept with a woman in months. I've never asked anyone to marry me before. I don't have any diseases. And I don't need your money."

"Oh," Lizzie breathed.

"I want to marry you," he said, offering the sentence as if it were merely a clarification. "But I can understand that you might not be ready to marry someone you've known two days. I can give you time. A week, perhaps."

"I hardly think that coaching needs to take this long," Cat called.

Oliver turned and jerked his head at Joshua in some sort of silent male exchange.

"They're forfeiting a turn," Joshua said. "Look, darling, that puts us one stroke ahead of Lizzie."

"We can't allow them to win," Lizzie whispered, but she didn't really care.

Oliver's hungry smile had nothing to do with the game. "We can afford to give up a stroke or two." He bent his head and kissed her again, kissed her until she felt stupid and slow, and fast and alive, all at the same time. Her pulse was galloping.

"Your turn again, Uncle Oliver," Hattie shrieked, some time later.

There was laughter in the girl's voice; obviously, they'd all seen what was happening. It was monstrously improper . . . and in front of children!

This time when Lizzie turned away, Oliver allowed it. She felt as if her brain had fried, like a cracked egg left in the sun on a hot day. She couldn't think of anything other than the fact that her cheeks must be bright red.

But no one said anything. She took her turn, followed by Cat. The girls' ball had rolled into a corner and they lost four strokes trying to get it out. Joshua was hovering, watching like a hawk to make certain that Hattie didn't cheat again.

They began begging for help and in the end, Oliver strode over and played their ball.

The mallet hung loosely from his hand as he bent slightly, showing the girls the proper form to play a game that he'd never even tried before that evening. He was wearing dove gray trousers, fashionable without being overly tight.

They were extremely flattering when he bent over. Lizzie discovered that she was fascinated by his legs—he had pushed a muscular thigh between her legs when they were kissing and the feeling . . .

Her pulse was thrumming in her throat, and she could tell that her hands were shaking, just slightly. She felt hot and restless, as if she wanted to throw the mallet to the floor.

When it was her turn again, Lizzie announced that she would play her turn alone. She was afraid that if Oliver wrapped himself around her, everyone would see her trembling.

There was a smile in the depths of Oliver's eyes that gave her a feeling of heating from the inside out. But he guided her through the next few strokes without touching her. They were within one stroke of winning and she was waiting for the girls to finish their turn when a horrid thought occurred to her.

Oliver knew she was a widow and of course he would think she was experienced in the bedroom. She swallowed hard, a familiar wash of shame coming over her like a warm blanket.

How could she explain that her husband had had no interest? That even when he attempted, he couldn't do the deed with her? What if—what if the same thing happened with Oliver?

She would die of shame. In fact—

A hand curled around her wrist and she jerked her head up.

"What's the matter?" Oliver asked in a low voice.

"I can't do it," she blurted out.

"What?"

"*That.*"

He took her mallet and leaned it against a chair. Then he called over to Joshua, "We're forfeiting the game."

Joshua let out a howl of laughter.

"We're winning," Lizzie protested.

Oliver's hand slid down her wrist and his fingers laced between hers.

"You won't leave the room with my sister," Cat said, appearing suddenly. "Because that would be most improper."

Lizzie opened her mouth to offer a protest, since she had no need for a chaperone, but Oliver simply said, "We're merely going to sit down and watch you play. Lady Troutt is tired."

Cat turned, and Lizzie knew all her exhausted, ashamed feelings were evident in her eyes.

Her sister's expression immediately changed. "Oh, Lizzie, you told me how exhausted you were, and I didn't listen. Do sit down, and I'll order some tea. Or would you prefer hot milk?"

"Neither," Lizzie said faintly. "Thank you."

She was going to have to tell Oliver the truth, no matter how humiliating it was. He wasn't a liar, and she refused to make up a falsehood, even if it spared her embarrassment. She would tell him the truth about her marriage.

Not only had Adrian not fallen in love with her, as her father had confidently predicted, he couldn't even perform in her presence.

"A glass of brandy," Oliver was saying. "Actually, two."

Lizzie meant to say that she didn't drink spirits, but she was trying to figure out how to make the most embarrassing confession of her life. Before she knew it, she and Oliver were tucked in a settee at the side of the room, sipping glasses of something that tasted like liquid fire while Cat bustled back to the game.

Unfortunately, it seemed that the girls had taken advantage of the interruption in play and nudged their ball into a better position.

"I feel I should apologize for my niece," Oliver said, after they sat for a moment in silence. "She's very young to be so criminally minded. I blame my sister's incessant Bible study."

Lizzie could feel anxiety beating in her bloodstream. "Your seduction," she said, and stopped.

Oliver was looking down at her. "I truly want to marry you," he said conversationally.

"No," she said with a gasp. "The only question is whether I would allow you to seduce me and I feel that I have to tell you that I may not suit you in bed."

He burst into laughter. It was the first time she'd heard Oliver laugh from his belly, a deep, rolling humor that made his face light up. It was the most sensual thing she'd ever seen.

Still.

"I mean it," she persisted.

"Why would you think such an absurdity?" he asked, managing to control his amusement.

"My marriage with Adrian was not consummated," she said, fidgeting with a fold of her gown.

She looked up just in time to see a bolt of pure joy cross Oliver's face.

Oh.

She hadn't thought about it from a man's point of view.

"At this point, little I can learn about your late husband would shock me. Still, that is most surprising. Why?"

"He was incapable with me," Lizzie said flatly. "I didn't have the kind of figure he admired, and I refused to do what he requested." Panic reared over her like an ocean wave. "I can't imagine why we're having this conversation. I must have been temporarily out of my mind to entertain the thought, Mr. Berwick."

"So Troutt had no lead in his pencil, hmmm?" Oliver's voice had a thread of pure wicked laughter running through it.

She frowned and then nodded, figuring out the reference. "Yes, that was the problem."

Oliver took a drink of his cognac. "I expect he carried too much weight." He turned toward her and before she jerked her eyes away, she caught sight of his powerful thighs, outlined by his silk pantaloons. There was no reason why that should cause a deep glow in her belly, but it did.

"What did you say?" she asked.

"Troutt was too fat, which was likely why he had a hanging Johnny, as we used to call it."

Fat? What did that have to do with it?

"That's not what he said." Lizzie really, truly, didn't want to repeat the things that Adrian had said to her. But she had to make one thing clear. "I won't do any of those things he requested," she stated. "Not to him or anyone."

Oliver grinned. "Let me guess. He wanted you to caress him or kiss him until he could manage a cock-stand?"

Her mind reeled, putting together "up" and "stand" with "cock" and "hanging."

Finally she nodded. "Something like that."

"I'm glad Troutt was incapable," Oliver said flatly.

"He wasn't *always* incapable. Only with me." It had to be said. "Obviously, he wasn't incapable with Sadie. She has—I gather she has a very large bosom."

Oliver muttered something profane that made the sting of Adrian's explanation ease away as if it had never been. "A man isn't incapable with a woman because of the size of her breasts, sweetheart," he said. "Especially one whose breasts are as beautiful as yours."

She was starting to feel foolish. She should have realized that. Her governess had often said that men were lascivious, with no reference to the size of one's bosom.

"I expect that Troutt blamed his problem on you because it's a humiliating thing for a man to be unable to consummate his own marriage," Oliver continued.

"Clearly, he could do it with Sadie. He had a child by her, a son."

Oliver made a *humphing* sound.

"Do you have any illegitimate sons?" she asked.

"Absolutely not."

That gave Lizzie such a sparkling jolt of happiness that she made a clean breast of it. "Sadie gave their child to an orphanage after Adrian died. What sort of mother does that? I disliked Adrian—there were times when I *hated* him—but I couldn't allow his son to grow up in an orphanage." She raised her glass and took a burning gulp of brandy.

"What did you do for the child?" Oliver asked. "I must admit that I find myself reluctant to raise Troutt's by-blow by way of Shady Sadie, but I will reconcile myself if the boy is part of your household."

Lizzie wrinkled her nose. "That would be going too far. I sold all of Adrian's property that wasn't entailed and set up a fund for him. The child now lives with a nice woman in the country."

"Troutt left no provision for his son?"

"I believe he thought that Sadie would raise the child out of affection."

Oliver was silent for a moment, thinking. Then he shook his head. "Actually, I don't think the boy was his child. My guess is that he needed Sadie to mask his incapacity."

Lizzie's mouth fell open. "Why on earth would you think that?"

"For all his idiocy, Troutt was a gentleman."

No *gentleman* would behave the way Adrian had.

"Gentleman by birth," Oliver clarified. "Troutt would have made provision for the child, had it been his. But more than that, he never consummated your marriage, Lizzie."

"I am quite aware," she said, keeping her chin high.

"If he could have managed it, he would have," Oliver said. His hands slipped down her back and he drew her against his chest, risking Cat's wrath. Then he bent his head and whispered, "There's no man on God's earth who wouldn't leap at the chance to make love to you."

LIZZIE WAS SMILING at Oliver, giving him a wide, beautiful smile, when the drawing room door burst open.

"The Earl of Mayne," Bartleby shouted, his chest puffed up importantly. "The Countess of Mayne, and Miss Cecily Langham."

Oliver didn't even turn in that direction. "May I seduce you, as a prelude to marrying you, my dearest Lizzie?"

She should tell him that she never meant to get married. But there was something about his eyes—so intent and honorable. "Seduction," she whispered. "Not marriage."

Oliver gave her a swift kiss, and stood up. "Shall we greet your sister's guests?"

Lizzie looked at his outstretched hand and shook her head. She needed to sit alone for a moment and think about their conversation. Oliver's surmise about Adrian changed everything she had believed about her marriage.

About herself.

She watched Oliver stride over to greet the earl and countess. It made sense that Adrian had lashed out at her to mask his own failures.

For a moment, she wondered about what sort of agreement her husband had had with Shady Sadie, and then she dismissed the thought. That wasn't her business. If Adrian had truly been a gentleman, he would have provided for the child, whether it was his or no. After all, the world thought it was his, and he'd shared a house with the boy for over a year.

But Adrian had been no gentleman. For the first time, instead of a blinding rage when she thought of her former husband, she felt nothing but withering contempt, along with a healthy dose of acceptance.

She should get up and greet her sister's guests, but instead she watched the earl talking to Joshua, as Oliver walked Lady Mayne over to the side of the room, his dark head bent as he spoke to her.

Making amends, Lizzie thought. He was a good man. Many people didn't care how they hurt other people.

She *would* allow herself be seduced by Oliver. Then she would go back to her house and all her books. It would wash away memory of Adrian's squinty eyes as he told her that her bosom wasn't enough for him.

The truth was the reverse.

He hadn't been enough for her. Any more than Shady Sadie had been, apparently.

She would no longer allow Adrian's loathing to define her. Obviously, Josie hadn't allowed the nickname "Scottish Sausage" to shape her life, any more than Cat had bothered about being called the Wooly Breeder.

Adrian's behavior was *his*, and it didn't reflect on her.

Lady Mayne was laughing at whatever Oliver was saying. She was very pretty, with lush curves and vivid, sparkling eyes.

She seemed to think that Oliver was funny; she was patting his cheek. As Lizzie watched, the earl appeared at his wife's shoulder, looking quite unfriendly.

Perhaps Lord Mayne disliked meeting one of the men who had caused his wife unhappiness. He pulled his countess back against his long body and gave Oliver a cold look.

Oliver must have known just how to diffuse the tension, because a few moments later the earl was also laughing. Only then did Lizzie realize that Mayne had responded to the fact his wife had touched Oliver's arm. Now that Lady Mayne was leaning back in her husband's arms, the earl stopped looking ferocious and seemed perfectly genial.

She kept watching as the earl turned in response to a

tug on his trousers. A governess stood beside him, holding hands with a beautiful little girl.

The earl instantly bent down and scooped the child into his arms. Mayne's daughter—Cecily, wasn't she?—leaned her head against her father's shoulder and began sucking her thumb.

Cecily had soft dark curls that rumpled against her father's shoulder as he held her tight, one hand making reassuring circles on her back. It was the kind of caress that made a little girl's eyes droop, because she felt safe and loved in her daddy's arms.

Lizzie felt tears prick her eyes, but they weren't the bitter tears she'd shed during the years of her marriage. She could remember her father's strong arms around her. He had made a terrible mistake, marrying her to Adrian and not supporting her when she pleaded for an annulment.

It was time to forgive him. She didn't feel like visiting him just yet, but she could write him a letter.

As she watched, Joshua and Sarah joined the group, Hattie tagging along. Neither Mayne nor Joshua would ever be unfaithful. Anyone could see that in the way they looked at their wives with fierce adoration and possessiveness. And a touch of reverence.

Well, perhaps that was going too far in the case of Joshua. No one could *revere* her older sister. Cat was too daft for that.

A hand tucked under her arm. "Come along, goose," Cat said fondly. "I want to introduce you to Josie. She's right there, so you can have no excuses."

"All right," Lizzie said, madly wishing that she had had time to brush her hair. The countess was so incredibly lovely, with glowing skin and a ruby mouth.

Cat tugged her forward. "I know what you're thinking," she whispered. "Everyone feels that way when they first meet Josie. You simply have to remember that she's the funniest, sweetest person you'll ever meet, and she hasn't the slightest idea of the effect she has on people."

Lizzie didn't want to know if Oliver was looking at Josie with desire in his eyes. "How can she not know?"

"She only notices her husband. Mayne told me that he had to marry her by special license in order to hold off all the men lusting after her."

"She's so lucky," Lizzie said with longing.

"Yes, she is," her sister said. "So am I. And Lizzie"—a distinctly mischievous note came into her voice—"I rather think that if you looked about you, you would discover that you could be that lucky as well."

Chapter Twelve

AFTER SHE RETIRED for the night, Lizzie took a bath and put on a delicate lawn nightgown that Cat had brought her from Paris. Then she sat down by the fire. Her hair was so curly that she had to finger-comb the strands to dry them.

How did an illicit rendezvous take place? Oliver had raised her hand to his lips when she said goodnight, and then asked quietly, eyes very bright, "Tonight, my lady?"

And she—risking the possibility of ending up in a "bad place" with butter-loving ants—had nodded.

Nodded!

She, Lizzie Troutt, was about to do something illicit. Disobedient. Cat had done naughty things when they were children, but Lizzie always looked to their father for reassurance and love, too timid to be disobedient.

Too afraid that she wouldn't be loved, if truth be told.

How would Oliver locate her bedchamber? Surely she

wasn't supposed to go to his? She hadn't the faintest idea where his chamber was.

She could hardly ask Cat. Her sister might have mischievously suggested that she should have had an *affaire* while married to Adrian, but she would be horrified to think that Lizzie would actually contemplate something so scandalous.

That made Lizzie grin.

By inviting a man to her bedchamber, she was being more wicked than Cat ever had. The very idea that Oliver might walk into her room any moment made a hot feeling spring up in her stomach again and—if she were honest—in her most private parts as well.

But the clock ticked on and after a while her hair was dry, hanging like a shining curtain between herself and the rest of the room.

Just when she was about to give up, braid her hair, and go to bed, the door silently opened and Oliver slipped through.

Lizzie sprang to her feet.

He had his hand on the door, as if he were about to close it. But when he saw her, he froze in place, a look on his face that was something like pain.

"Good evening," she managed, knowing it was an absurd thing to say.

Slowly, slowly, he closed the door behind him and leaned back against it. He cleared his throat. "Jesus. You're exquisite, Lizzie."

Her mouth wobbled into a smile. Oliver swallowed so hard that she could see his throat move, and that made her *feel* beautiful.

She also felt awkward, shy, and incredibly embarrassed.

"Mayne was in a talkative mood," he said, not moving. "His stables and his wife. His wife and his stables. I thought he'd never shut up. I actually thought about knocking him out. Quick mallet to the head and he'd be sleeping like a baby."

"I'm glad you didn't," she managed.

He began walking toward her with controlled grace, the stride that signaled his prowess at croquet and likely all other kinds of sports as well.

She could feel herself getting even redder as she took that thought to its obvious conclusion.

"I'm afraid I won't be good at this," she blurted out, when he was almost close enough to touch her.

His eyes drifted down her body and it suddenly occurred to Lizzie that she was standing in front of the fire and likely the thin lawn of her nightgown had left her every curve exposed.

"I think you're going to be a natural," Oliver said, stopping just before her and bending his head to kiss her. His eyes had gone darker, cobalt blue now.

There was something about kissing Oliver that made all her nervousness and fear melt away. She didn't even pretend to feel maidenly hesitation. His mouth touched hers, her lips opened, and her tongue met his. A quake of fire went through her body.

Kissing wasn't at all what she'd imagined. She'd seen men and women press their lips together in a salutation that looked pleasant but unhygienic.

This was raw and sensual, and at the same time, familiar. Necessary. Kissing Oliver was like water and food.

With a half-sob, half-moan, she fell into his arms. He held her tightly, his tongue gliding deep into her mouth, making her whole being throw off sparks as if she were a Chinese sparkler, one of the ones that she'd seen in London on Guy Fawkes Day.

So she wound her arms around his neck and held on, her mind going blank and silent even as her body registered the strength of his arms, the hard planes of his body against the melting softness of hers, the little growl that came from his throat when she pressed closer.

That safe feeling she had around Oliver doubled and redoubled as they kissed, one kiss blending into the next, separated only by a whispered word or two, a quick breath. His lips skimmed her cheeks, pressed a kiss on her eyelid, but their mouths kept coming back together.

Some kisses began chastely, like a warm reassurance. They gave her time to collect herself, because needy, hard kisses made her tremble so hard that she was frightened by her own reaction. The sting between her legs, the heat and throb of her feelings, sent qualms of terror through her.

As if Oliver knew, somehow, when she was overbalancing into fear, his kisses would turn warm but respectful, letting her set the pace.

After a while, she would gather courage and press closer, opening her mouth wider, her tongue meeting his. Oliver would give a muffled sound, a curse, a groan, and their kiss would build to a wildfire again.

Still his hands never strayed lower than her back, though she felt an edgy, sharp awareness that she wanted him to touch her there . . . everywhere.

When he didn't move his hands, it allowed her to be bold. She let her hands stray down his wide back. He was wearing only a shirt, waistcoat, and breeches, and she could feel thick cords of muscles under her fingertips.

She felt as much as heard a growl deep in his throat as she caressed him. She ran her fingers up the bunched strength of his stomach muscles, her fingers splaying wide on his chest, her hands crushed between their bodies as he pulled her even closer, ravishing her mouth, licking and sucking and even biting at her.

There was a hot brand pressing against her stomach, an unmistakable sign that Oliver wanted her. No: that he was desperate for her. She shook at the realization, a whimper breaking from her lips.

He wanted her so much that his breathing was labored. His fingers trembled on her back. His big male body was poised over her, around her, like a cocked pistol—and yet he kept still for her. So as not to frighten her.

Blindly she sought his mouth again, sliding her tongue between his lips like a woman who knew what she wanted, at the same moment her body melted against his hot shaft, cradling his hard thigh between her legs, pushing at him with an unspoken demand.

Instantly, he pulled away, cradling her face in his hands. "Lizzie," he breathed.

"Yes?" Her voice was a siren's whisper that couldn't belong to her.

"I don't want to seduce you."

The words went down her body like a shock of cold water, a sickening shock of dismay and misgiving. She pulled back, swallowed. Why had he been kissing her? Why was he in her room?

Her mind reeled: was he put off by the way she kissed? Or the way she pressed against his body? She had been too insistent. It wasn't ladylike. Or—

He tipped up her chin and the look in his eyes made the windmill shudder to a halt. "Whatever it is that you're thinking, *stop*. You can't think that I don't want you."

"Well," she said with a little gasp, "Well, then . . ."

"I don't want to seduce you like this, secretly, behind people's backs."

"Why not?" At this precise moment, she wouldn't care if half the county knew he was in her room.

"It's not right."

"I can't be ruined," she pointed out. "I'm a widow. And you said that—you promised that you would seduce me."

"I don't want an *affaire*."

She shook her head, not believing him. "You don't?"

He clutched her, his big hands warm on her shoulders. "I didn't say that right. God, I want you so badly that I might lose control for the first time since I was fourteen."

Lizzie wasn't sure what he meant, but a smile trembled on her lips.

He let go and dragged a hand through his hair. "I can't make love to you like this, in secret. Damn it, I want you to be my bride!"

The truth that she had honed and polished in her

mind over the miserable years of her marriage slipped out of her mouth. "I don't plan to marry, ever again."

His hands slid down her arms. "Why not?"

"A wife is no more than a possession, a thing. She has no rights, she has no money, she has nothing. She *is* nothing."

Oliver brought her right hand up to his mouth and pressed a warm kiss onto her palm. "You would never be nothing to me. Never. You're everything to me."

"I would be your possession, legally and otherwise." Lizzie bit her lip. "I want to be free. I like you. I truly do."

She stopped because something painful flashed through his eyes.

"I believe I feel something more than that for you," he said, his tone oddly courteous, like that of a medieval knight. "I seem to have fallen in love with you, Lizzie Troutt."

She blinked up at him. "That's impossible."

A corner of his mouth tipped upward. "Why?"

"You scarcely know me."

He cocked his head. "I feel as if I've known you my entire life. I have never asked another woman to marry me; I've never even considered it. Yet I saw you, Lizzie, and within a day, I wanted to put a ring on your finger."

Lizzie realized she was gaping, and snapped her mouth shut. "That's impossible."

"You're beautiful. No, you're more than beautiful. You're exquisite. You're intelligent, wry, and funny; you like to read; you don't like fancy balls, but you like to ride, even though I haven't seen you on a horse yet; you have an incredible waist; your hips are even better; your mouth drives me crazy; your eyes are beautiful; I want to make you laugh."

"Oh," she breathed.

"I want to make you laugh, and I want to make sure you eat. I want to see you limp and sweaty and pleasured on my bed. If you don't want howling plums in the house, that's fine, but I would love a little girl with your mouth and all that hair. It was all I could think about when I watched Mayne holding his baby girl. I want you, Lizzie, in my life, and in my bed, and anywhere else you'll have me."

Her eyes searched his face. He was a man who said what he thought, directly. You could trust him to tell the truth.

"You don't ever take advantage of people, do you?" she asked.

A look of distaste cross his face. "No."

"Your sister is doing so." It hadn't escaped her that Adrian had dumped her on his mother because he needed a caretaker, and Oliver's sister had done the same with her own daughter.

"My sister is my family. And I love Hattie. She's a royal pain, but I still love her." His large hands caressed her back, tempting her to sink forward into his arms again.

Lizzie swallowed hard. Oliver was such a good man, and it was so ironic that they met because he came to apologize for doing something unkind.

If she married him, he would never be unkind. She knew it in her bones.

"I don't have any money," she said, her eyes fixed on his so she could see if there was even a trace of disappointment. "I gave it all to Sadie's son, and my jointure was very small."

No disappointment.

"I have no need for money. I only need you." His voice was achingly honest.

Lizzie stepped back so his hands fell to his sides. She couldn't think when he was touching her. Oliver's hair tumbled over his brow; he would never bother with an elegant hairstyle.

"Do you have a valet?" she asked.

"No."

He didn't apologize or explain. He just waited for her to make a decision, his dark blue eyes steady, seeming to realize that she had to think it out.

"I don't like eating six courses, and I read too many books, and I am easily bored."

He nodded. "All right."

"Perhaps this would be a good idea, and perhaps it wouldn't."

"Why wouldn't it?"

"We may not suit, on coming to know each other better."

"You suit me," he said simply. "I know it. I will do my best to suit you."

There was something about his bluntness that made her heart sing. It made her knees weak, even more so when Oliver began to deftly untie his neck cloth, exposing the strong neck that she had ogled earlier in the day.

Lizzie pulled her mind back to the topic at hand. Never mind the fact that he had unbuttoned one of his cuffs, and was working on the other.

Just as if—well, as if they were married. As if he'd come to her chamber after supper with family, and an impromptu game of croquet, and . . .

He was pulling off his waistcoat.

"Are you undressing?" she said weakly.

"I am," he said, taking off his boots and then his stockings. Lizzie discovered that she was fascinated by his feet. They were so long, and powerful looking, and yet somehow graceful.

Something flashed in the corner of her eye, and she looked up. His shirt was gone. She let her eyes drop from the powerful column of Oliver's throat down to his shoulders, down further to the wide arc of his chest. His body narrowed to a waist that rippled with muscle, a light furring leading to the top of his pantaloons.

Her heart was beating in her chest with a ferocity driven by lust. She wanted to touch him, caress him. *Lick* him.

She gulped, a small sound in the quiet room. His eyes were raw with desire and yet tender as well.

"I suppose I could try marriage again," she said shakily. Her eyes darted over his body.

He was laughing again, not as loudly as before, but joyfully. "I would be very grateful to seduce you—and to wed you. I've had a cockstand since about five minutes after I met you. It's starting to hurt."

His stomach muscles rippled as he laughed, which

was one of the most enticing things she'd ever seen in her life.

"Really?" she squeaked.

"When I walked into the drawing room two days ago, I was focused on meeting Cat. But I registered that you were gorgeous. Then you didn't come down to breakfast the next day. I waited for an hour, pretending to read the paper."

"I was afraid."

He walked closer, bent his head and brushed his lips across hers. "Don't ever be afraid of me, sweetheart."

"I won't," she said with a gulp, feeling the strength of that promise reverberate through her bones.

"May I take these breeches off? They no longer fit . . . they've become bloody uncomfortable, as a matter of fact."

It was a moment of decision, Lizzie supposed, and yet there was nothing to decide. He was hers, or she was his . . .

Possession was not what she thought it was.

"I'll do it for you," she whispered. She ducked her head, and her hair tumbled forward. Corkscrew curls ranging in color from pale sunshine to wheat fell over Oliver's arms as he steadied her, falling over her hands as she fumbled at his waistband.

She found the top button inside his placket. His trousers were strained because of—well, because. It made it difficult to work the button through.

His hands drifted over her shoulders and down her front, shaping a tender caress. "Your breasts are the perfect size for my hands," he murmured.

She looked up.

"May I?" he asked.

She frowned, puzzled. "Yes?"

With one swift movement, he ripped her French nightgown open to the waist.

"There they are," he breathed, his voice reverent, dark.

Lizzie looked down absorbing what she saw. She *was* just the right size for his hands: not too big, not too little. Oliver bent his head and captured one of her nipples, making her cry out in startled pleasure.

One of his hands slid to her waist, holding her still so that he could ravish first one breast, then the other, making her breath come in little pants.

"Oliver," she whimpered, as a callused thumb rubbed over her breast, making her knees almost buckle. "I . . ."

"Lizzie, sweetheart." He pulled back, the light in his eyes so ferocious that he resembled a wild beast. And yet that huge body was contained, at her service.

"You don't think my mouth is too large?" she blurted out.

When Oliver roared with laugher, she spread her hands flat on his abdomen because it was enticing to be able to feel laughter as well as hear it.

"Your mouth is most tempting thing I've ever seen," he said, once he quieted. There was a raw quality to his voice that told her he was telling the truth.

Again.

Always.

Smiling, she went back to wrestling with his trouser placket, working the second button free, eliciting a groan when her fingers brushed his shaft.

Oliver removed her hand from his trousers and ripped open his placket himself. "I can't take it any longer."

Lizzie couldn't think straight, not when he was shoving his trousers down his legs and his tool was springing forward.

"Look at yourself," he commanded.

She glanced down. Breasts, waist, hips—her nightgown had caught on them, thank goodness—below that, pink toes. Plus pale curls falling over her shoulders and cascading almost to her waist.

Then, like magic, she saw herself through his eyes: slender but rounded, sensual shadows and curves, hair that enticed, hiding her nipples. An erotic body.

"It's as if someone knew my innermost desires, and shaped you only for me," he said hoarsely.

Lizzie brushed her hair behind her shoulders, hearing the stifled noise he made and loving it.

She gave a little wiggle and a desperate, raw groan broke from Oliver's lips.

As she pushed down her nightgown, a shadowed patch of curls appeared, along with legs that were so slender that her thighs seemed plump in comparison.

Oliver didn't say a word. He just stood before her, offering bold evidence of his arousal.

Aroused by her. By her body. By herself.

She would never again think of herself as an unattractive country mouse. She realized, with a thrill that went to the bottom of her toes, that she had found a man just like her brother-in-law.

Just like the Earl of Mayne.

A man who was possessive in good ways, but not in

bad. Who would love and shelter her, but also encourage and embolden her.

Oliver scooped her up and lay her on the bed. Thinking about what would make him happy, Lizzie decided to be bold. Her hands drifted over his body until he opened heavy-lidded eyes and growled, "I'm sorry, Lizzie. I can't take it any longer or I will shame myself."

Excitement caught in her throat and blocked any words, but she nodded. His heavy body arched over hers and he began kissing her, starting at her breasts, sliding lower to her stomach, lower still.

"Are you sure about that?" she asked in alarm.

But he was sure, murmuring something about honey and flowers. His tongue slid down her inner thighs as his roughened thumb dragged down her most sensitive parts and she stiffened all over, toes curling as a sheet of flame swept through her body.

"Oliver!" she cried. Her fingers curled in his hair, holding him in place. He made a rumbling approving sound, licked her again, and thrust a broad finger into her.

Just like that, Lizzie felt herself convulsing, crying out in bliss, her body curling up toward him. Sweat sprang out all over her body, but he didn't stop, he kept kissing her, murmuring about how beautiful she was, and one erotic spasm swept straight into the next and she was tightening around his finger all over again, sobbing this time, her fingers pulling his hair.

"Come here, come here," she cried, hands sliding over his shoulders, pulling at him. Finally his body hovered over hers again, and he began sliding inside her.

He was large, too large.

They had to stop while she caught her breath. She wiggled, and discovered how good that felt.

Stopped again—he groaned and dropped his forehead onto hers—while she decided whether she felt like a bottle with a cork.

Or whether there was something amazing happening, some liquid, excruciating torment.

Her body decided for her, pushing up against him, seating him deep in the tight clasp of her body.

"Please," she cried, forgetting anything but this, the feeling of completion and heat and madness. "Oliver!"

With a deep grunt, he took over. Poised above her on his elbows, kissing her until heat began climbing up her limbs again and she turned her face because she had to breathe—she'd forgotten how to breathe—she had to shriek.

She did shriek as his hot length drove deep into her body, over and over. Oliver's shuddering inability to control himself was like oil thrown on a fire: she arched like a bow beneath him, her body breaking apart and reforming into something new.

Part of that new Lizzie lived for Oliver, woke at Oliver's touch, sang at the way he thrust one last time, a harsh sound torn from his throat . . . then collapsed on top of her, crushing her.

They were sweaty and slippery. The room rang with the silent echo of their cries. The bed had lost everything but the bottom sheet.

Oliver had never known it, but when a woman breaks

into a laugh while a man is still inside her, it's an aphrodisiac like no other. A joyful laugh is reinvigorating, even if that man has just made love—really made love—for the first time in his life.

He kissed Lizzie and then asked for the sixth or seventh time if she would marry him.

No, he demanded it, and this time, she said yes. Then they made love all night, tender, passionate, crazed.

The next morning, he dragged his future wife out of bed, sleepily protesting, out to the stables, onto a horse.

Then, when she proved to be a trifle sore, he took her onto his lap and kissed her as his mount meandered through a meadow, going wherever he willed.

Lizzie never knew exactly why Oliver took her out in the dawn light. It had something to do with her sister. She didn't know why he kept tickling her and making her laugh so hard that she almost fell off the horse a few times.

"I always wanted to make love in a field," he told her, perfectly seriously.

She felt her eyes go round. "In a *field*?"

"Yes, in a field, and then return to the house and get married."

"*What*?"

"Did I forget to mention that Joshua took a carriage last night to fetch a marriage license from the Bishop of Chichester?" His smile was the wicked, sleepy smile of a reformed rake. "It's his first act as my future brother-in-law. We'll marry in St. Mary's church in Walberton, Lizzie, just as soon as you'll have me."

"Oh," she breathed. She could cry . . . or she could laugh.

Laughter is a medicine that cures the greatest anguish, mends the sharpest humiliation, cures the soul.

So she laughed.

Epilogue

YOUNG MASTER BERWICK was born on an early spring morning, approximately nine months after his parents met.

It had been a mercifully quick birth, which meant that his mother and father were able to focus on their new baby, rather than collapsing in exhaustion.

Mostly they stared at him. In fact, if he had but known it, that would quickly become one of their favorite occupations.

Mind you, their comments were not always complimentary.

"How's the plum today?" was a common question.

Except they both knew precisely how the plum was, since they couldn't seem to stay away from the nursery.

They had to replace one well-recommended nanny be cause she believed in foolish ideas such as children being presented in the drawing room for a half-hour only, and otherwise kept to a strict routine in the nursery.

That wouldn't have allowed the plum to go out in the pony cart, or to be taken on picnics so that his cousin Hattie could tickle him until he turned purple from laughing so much. It wouldn't have allowed his mother to find a shady spot in the gardens, and breastfeed her baby while she read the latest novel.

Or his father to find the two of them, and throw himself down on the blanket and watch, waiting until the plum fell asleep, looking as round and fat and plum-like as only a much-nurtured, much-loved, and much-fed baby can look.

That allowed his parents to work on their next project, a little plumlet to go with the plum.

"This one will have your hair," Oliver murmured.

Lizzie was laughing, the sound drifting across the gardens. "How can you be so sure? Cat's three children all have Joshua's hair, and look at the plum. Your hair, exactly."

Oliver had built a little tent over the baby so that if his son awoke, he wouldn't be shocked by parental frolicking. He had lulled his wife with kisses and whispered compliments and hungry caresses.

He had managed to slide her gown up to where he wanted it, past her plump thighs and still slender hips, though she ate considerably better now that they'd found a cook who understood vegetables.

"I just know," he said.

And he was right.

A Note About Croquet and Countesses

CAT AND JOSHUA'S game of croquet was, obviously, played in an unlikely location. A young gentry family would have played it on the lawn, although they wouldn't necessarily have called by that name. The first mention of croquet in the *Oxford English Dictionary* comes from a citation in 1858. But the OED notes that croquet resembles the ancient game of *closh*, as well as pall-mall, also known as *paille-maille*, which was a popular outdoor game in England by the 1600s. All three of these games involved hitting a ball with a mallet through and around obstacles, though none, I would venture to say, were played with the bravado and gaiety of the young Windingham household.

Josie, the Countess of Mayne, and her husband, the Earl of Mayne appear in all four of my series about the Essex sisters. Josie and Mayne's love story was spurred by the fact that her nickname, the "Scottish Sausage," appeared likely to ruin her matrimonial chances—at least until Mayne taught her what men truly like about women's figures. Their story begins with *Much Ado About You*, excerpted below.

And if you're curious about the mention of "Silly Billy"—a pejorative that was not made up by Darlington and Berwick, but is in the same cruel vein—you can find a short story, "A Midsummer Night's Disgrace," in the *Essex Sisters Companion Guide*; a peek at this novella follows the excerpt of *Much Ado*.

Read on for an excerpt from

Much Ado About You

**the first novel in the Essex Sisters quartet.
Available wherever books are sold!**

September 1816
Holbrook Court, seat of the Duke of Holbrook
On the outskirts of Silchester

In the afternoon

"I AM HAPPY to announce that the rocking horses have been delivered, Your Grace. I have placed them in the nursery for your inspection. As yet, there is no sign of the children."

Raphael Jourdain, Duke of Holbrook, turned. He had been poking a fire smoldering in the cavernous fireplace of his study. There was a reserved tone in his butler's voice that signaled displeasure. Or perhaps it would be more accurate to say that Brinkley's tone signaled the disgruntlement of the entire household of elderly servants, not one of whom was enchanted by the idea of accommodating themselves to the presence of four small, female children. Well, the hell with that, Rafe thought. It wasn't as if he'd *asked* to have a passel of youngsters on the premises.

"Rocking horses?" came a drawling voice from a

deep chair to the right of the fireplace. "Charming, Rafe. Charming. One can't start too early making the little darlings interested in horseflesh." Garret Langham, the Earl of Mayne, raised his glass toward his host. His black curls were in exquisite disarray, his comments arrogant to a fault, and his manners barely hid a seething fury. Not that he was furious at Rafe; Mayne had been in a slow burn for the past few months. "To Papa and his brood of infant *equestriennes*," he added, tossing back his drink.

"Stubble it!" Rafe said, but without much real animosity. Mayne was a damned uncomfortable companion at the moment, what with his poisonous comments and black humor. Still, one had to assume that the foul temper caused by the shock of being rejected by a woman would wear off in a matter of time.

"Why the plural, as in rocking *horses*?" Mayne asked. "As I recall, most nurseries contain only one rocking horse."

Rafe took a gulp of his brandy. "I don't know much about children," he said, "but I distinctly remember my brother and me fighting over our toys. So I bought four of them."

There was a second's silence during which the earl considered whether to acknowledge the fact that Rafe obviously still missed his brother (dead these five years, now). He dismissed the impulse. Manlike, he observed no benefit to maudlin conversation.

"You're doing those orphans proud," he said instead. "Most guardians would stow the children out of sight. It's not as if they're your blood."

"There's no amount of dolls in the world that will make up for their situation," Rafe said, shrugging. "Their father should have thought of his responsibilities before he climbed on a stallion."

The conversation was getting dangerously close to the sort of emotion to be avoided at all costs, so Mayne sprang from his chair. "Let's have a look at the rocking horses, then. I haven't seen one in years."

"Right," Rafe said, putting his glass onto the table with a sharp clink. "Brinkley, if the children arrive, bring them upstairs, and I'll receive them in the nursery."

A few minutes later the two men stood in the middle of a large room on the third floor, dizzily painted with murals. Little Bo Peep chased after Red Riding Hood, who was surely in danger of being crushed by the giant striding across the wall, his raised foot lowering over a feather bed sporting a huge green pea under the coverlet. The room resembled nothing so much as a Bond Street toy shop. Four dolls with spun gold hair sat primly on a bench. Four doll beds were propped atop each other, next to four doll tables, on which sat four jack-in-the-boxes. In the midst of it all was a group of rocking horses graced with real horsehair and coming almost to a man's waist.

"Jesus," Mayne said.

Rafe strode into the room and stamped on the rocker of one of the horses, making it clatter back and forth on the wooden floor. A door on the side of the room swung open, and a plump woman in a white apron poked her head out.

"There you are, Your Grace," she said, beaming.

"We're just waiting for the children. Would you like to meet the new maids now?"

"Send them on in, Mrs. Beeswick."

Four young nursemaids crowded into the room after her. "Daisy, Gussie, Elsie, and Mary," said the nanny. "They're from the village, Your Grace, and pleased to have a position at Holbrook Court. We're all eager for the little cherubs to arrive." The nursemaids lined up to either side of Mrs. Beeswick, smiling and curtsying.

"Jesus," Mayne repeated. "They won't even share a maid, Rafe?"

"Why should they? My brother and I had three nurses between us."

"Three?"

"Two for my brother, ever since he turned duke at age seven, and one for me."

Mayne snorted. "That's absurd. When's the last time you met your wards' father, Lord Brydone?"

"Not for years," Rafe said, picking up a jack-in-the-box and pressing the lever so that it hopped from its box with a loud squeak. "The arrangement was just a matter of a note from him and my reply."

"You have never met your own wards?"

"Never. I haven't been over the border in years, and Brydone only came down for the Ascot, the Silchester, and, sometimes, Newmarket. To be honest, I don't think he really gave a damn for anything other than his stables. He didn't even bother to list his children in *Debrett's*. Of course, since he had four girls, there was no question of inheritance. The estate went to some distant cousin."

"Why on earth—" Mayne glanced at the five women standing to the side of the room and checked himself.

"He asked me," Rafe said, shrugging. "I didn't think twice of it. Apparently Monkton had been in line, but he cocked up his toes last year. And Brydone asked me to step in. Who would have thought that ill could come to Brydone? It was a freak accident, that horse throwing him. Although he was fool enough to ride a half-broken stallion."

"Damned if I thought I'd ever see you a father," Mayne said.

"I had no excuse to say no. I have the substance to raise any number of children. Besides, Brydone gave me Starling in return for acting as a guardian. I told him I'd do the job, as soon as he wrote me, and no bribe was necessary. But he sent Starling down from Scotland, and no one would say nay to adding that horse to their stables."

"Starling is out of Standout, isn't he?"

Rafe nodded. "Patchem's brother. The core of Brydone's stable is out of Patchem, and those are now the only horses in England in Patchem's direct line. I'm hopeful that Starling will win the Derby next year, even if he is descended from Standout rather than Patchem himself."

"What will happen to Patchem's offspring?" Mayne asked, with the particular intensity he reserved for talk of horses. "Something Wanton, for example?"

"I don't know yet. Obviously, the stables aren't entailed. My secretary has been up there working on the estate. Should Brydone's stable come to the children, I'll put the horses up for auction and the money in trust. The girls will need dowries someday, and I'd be surprised if Brydone bothered to set them up himself."

"If Wanton is for sale, I'm the one to buy him. I'd pay thousands for him. There could be no better addition to my stables."

"He would do wonders for mine as well," Rafe agreed.

Mayne had found a little heap of cast-iron horses and was sorting them out so that each carriage was pulled by a matched pair. "You know, these are quite good." He had all the cast-iron horses and their carriages lined up on the mantelpiece now. "Wait till your wards see these horses. They won't think twice about the move from Scotland. Pity there's no boy among them."

Rafe just looked at him. The earl was one of his dearest friends, and always would be. But Mayne's sleek, protected life had not put him in the way of grief. Rafe knew only too well what it felt like to find oneself lonely in the midst of a cozy nursery, and cast-iron horses wouldn't help, for all he found himself buying more and more of them. As if toys would make up for a dead father. "I hardly think you—"

The door behind him swung open. He stopped and turned.

Brinkley moved to the side more nimbly than was his practice. It wasn't every day that one got to knock the master speechless with surprise. "I'm happy to announce Miss Essex. Miss Imogen. Miss Annabel. Miss Josephine."

Then he added, unable to resist, if the truth be known, "The children have arrived, Your Grace."

Read on for an excerpt from

A Midsummer Night's Disgrace

from *The Official Essex Sisters Companion Guide*
Available now from Avon Books!

June 21, 1819
A House Party
Kent
Seat of the Duke of Ormond

"I DON'T UNDERSTAND what I did wrong," Lady Bellingworth moaned, wringing her hands. "You had the best governesses money could buy, and I took you to church often, and certainly every Easter!"

"You did your best, Mama," Cecilia replied. She spun in place, causing her new gown to swirl around her feet. "Isn't it *beautiful*?"

The gown was better described by what it wasn't: it wasn't white, demure, or ruffled. It didn't have the new gathered sleeves; in fact, it didn't have any sleeves. There wasn't much of a bodice either.

A fold of strawberry-colored silk wound around Cecilia's bosom and draped over her arms. Rather than following the line of her narrow skirts—made from a darker shade—the transparent overskirt clung to her hips before belling out around her toes. A row of embroidered strawberries around the hem weighted the over-skirt so it swirled around her as she moved, emphasizing her curves.

And she had them.

Cecilia considered her curves to be her best feature, with golden hair the color of old guineas a close second.

Coaxed into tight ringlets by a curling iron, her hair took on an oddly metallic gleam. But tonight her maid had styled it in a frothy pile of natural curls, stuck about with ruby-tipped hairpins.

"What are you wearing on your feet?" her mother cried, sounding rather like a kettle coming to boil.

Cecilia lifted her skirts and looked happily at her toes. "New shoes."

Lady Bellingworth turned purple. "Those are your great-aunt Margaret's diamond buckles!"

Her shoes were made of strawberry silk embroidered in a silver crosshatch pattern that went splendidly with diamond buckles. But the pièce de résistance was her heels. They were covered in strawberry-colored silk and guaranteed to catch the eye.

Generally speaking, ladies drifted around the ball-room in soft slippers, just as Cecilia had throughout the season. But she had carefully planned—in collusion with a brilliant modiste—to change her appearance from head to toe.

In the past two seasons, she had dutifully worn white (which didn't suit her), sat demurely at the sides of ball-rooms (which didn't suit her), and smiled rather than spoke (which really didn't suit her).

But she had arrived at the Duchess of Ormond's house party this afternoon without a single white gown in her baggage. When a Bellingworth decides to change her appearance, she doesn't hold back.

She was not going to drift around the ballroom: she would *sway*, and her hips would sway right along with her.

"You won't be able to dance in those shoes," her mother moaned.

"I shan't need to dance," Cecilia said, adroitly avoiding the issue, because in her opinion, the shoes turned a simple country dance step into an invitation. "The duchess announced a musical evening, remember, Mama? By the way, if we don't go down to the ballroom immediately, we shall be late for the concert."

Lady Bellingworth was slumped against the high back of the settee, hand over her heart. "I feel ill, positively ill. I cannot believe that my daughter is so lost to impropriety that she would consider wearing this . . . this costume better suited to the demimonde than a house party given by one of my oldest friends."

"If I were one of those ladies," Cecilia pointed out, "I would take off this corset, which is horribly uncomfortable."

"Do you think to find a husband this way?" her mother demanded. "To entice a gentleman to wed you because your gown is small enough to cram into his pocket?"

"Marriage would be desirable outcome, don't you think?" Cecilia asked. "My second season as a wallflower was more than enough."

She was tired of being ignored, tired of sitting at the side of the room watching other girls curtsying. She was tired of pity dances with male relatives, and whispered advice from girls younger than she was.

She had an idea that gentlemen didn't bother to look very closely at the rows of debutantes, because every young lady was dressed precisely the same. Swathed in white and trained to docility, they were no more distinct than one sheep in a flock.

"I know why you're doing this," her mother said, reaching up to pull Cecilia down onto the settee at her side. Her eyes had turned misty. "It's because of that dreadful nickname, isn't it? It's because poor James is called 'Silly Billy.' It's all my fault! There must have been something I could have done."

There was no question but that Cecilia's failure on the marriage market was wrapped up with the cruel, persistent jest about her brother, Lord Bellingworth, who had been dropped on his head as a baby. No one believed the truth about his injury. They thought that the Bellingworth blood was tainted and her babies would be silly as well.

She had a respectable dowry, excellent lineage, and even better teeth. She had shining hair, a slender waist, and slightly larger breasts than were normal for a young lady. But her second season had just drawn to a close, and she had had no suitors, not even one. "It's all just so *foolish*," her mother continued, mopping her eyes. "Poor James was perfectly normal until he suffered that terrible blow. Perfectly normal!"

"There's nothing you could have done, Mama," Cecilia said, wrapping her arm around her mother. "You have no control over the fools who rule the so-called Beau Monde. Darlington and his ilk."

"Charles Darlington didn't create that despicable nickname. It came from a horrid fellow known as Eliot Thurman, who was part of his circle a few years ago."

"I've heard as much," Cecilia said absently. She caught sight of her gown in the dressing table mirror and eased her bodice a bit lower, tugging down that blasted corset while she was at it.

It was French and hoisted her breasts in the air like a gift, but it was deucedly uncomfortable.

Luckily, her mother didn't notice what she was doing. "Thurman dropped out of society, and then of course, Darlington married Lady Griselda . . ."

Lady Bellingworth kept talking and talking until Cecilia finally intervened. "I think that people are fools to pay attention to people like Darlington. He published that fictional memoir about Josie's husband, the Earl of Mayne, after all. Josie says the earl doesn't mind, but I think it was rude."

"I know Josie, I mean the Countess of Mayne, is one of your closest friends, darling, but you should also remember that Lady Griselda is married to Darlington, and *she* is something of a stepmother to Lady Mayne," her mother said, tracing the twisty paths of society connections. "Besides, I like Darlington. He's apologized to me a hundred times, if not more, for having brought Thurman into society."

"Thurman may have invented 'Silly Billy,' but it took a whole herd of simpletons to repeat it over and over, turning my brother into a pariah."

"I am not defending Thurman," her mother said. "I loathe the man. Someone told me that he'd been shipped off to the Antipodes, though I don't know how accurate the rumor is."

"Mama, if we don't go downstairs, we'll be late," Cecilia said again, drawing her mother to her feet. She picked up a wisp of silk tulle and wound it around her shoulders.

"You're not pretending that scrap of fabric is a shawl!"

Cecilia put on an innocent expression. "Whatever can you mean? Madame Rocque fashioned it specifically for this gown."

"I recognize that look, you know," her mother said suddenly. "You had the same expression when you stole out of the house at twelve years old and begged that violin player to take you with him to Vienna." Her mother shuddered. "I've never forgotten the horror of it."

All Cecilia remembered was the disappointment. The violin player in question was Franz Clement, one of the best violinists in the world. Her attempt to persuade him to take her with him, back to Europe, had been the only time in her life, before this, that she had attempted to live life on her own terms.

She had failed, and in retrospect, she had to agree that the whole idea had been mad. Clement allowed her to play a Beethoven adagio and then promptly escorted her back to their London townhouse. "She'd be good enough if she were a man," he had told her mother.

"She's a lady!" her mother had retorted, in pure horror.

"Precisely," Clement had said, bowed, and left.

Now Cecilia turned to her mother. "I'm not threatening to run away from home this time, Mama. I've done nothing more outrageous than commission new gowns."

"I suppose we have no choice at this point," her mother said, as tragically as any Cleopatra. "I might as well face the humiliation now, as wait for London."

"It can't be more humiliating than having a wallflower as a daughter," Cecilia pointed out.

"Oh, how little you know of the world," her mother said grimly.

About the Author

ELOISA JAMES is a *New York Times* bestselling author and professor of English literature who lives with her family in New York, but can sometimes be found in Paris or Italy. She is the mother of two and, in a particularly delicious irony for a romance writer, is married to a genuine Italian knight. Visit her at www.eloisajames.com.

Discover great authors, exclusive offers, and more at hc.com.